Just as Mary took the last [...] concrete below, a bullet crashed through the door.

Walker swung onto the ladder, then jumped off the minute he was close enough to the ground to not break a leg. Then grabbed her hand and pulled her down the alley toward his car.

She tugged her hand from his grasp. He kept expecting her to break into fear or panic, but she was filled with nothing but a cool kind of skepticism as she looked at his car. "I don't believe I should go with you."

"Maybe you'd like to go with the guys shooting at me instead?" He tossed his bags in the back—except one gun he put in the middle console for easy reach. They had a minute, tops, before the bullets started again. "This car leaves in three seconds," he told her before closing his door.

She was in the passenger side—and buckled up of all things—in two.

"Keep low," he instructed. "They're going to follow. Hold on."

COLD CASE SCANDAL

NICOLE HELM

INTRIGUE

For oldest daughters and organized souls.

Harlequin® INTRIGUE™

ISBN-13: 978-1-335-59170-8

Cold Case Scandal

Copyright © 2024 by Nicole Helm

Harlequin Enterprises ULC
22 Adelaide St. West, 41st Floor
Toronto, Ontario M5H 4E3, Canada
www.Harlequin.com

Printed in Lithuania

MIX
Paper | Supporting responsible forestry
FSC® C021394

Nicole Helm grew up with her nose in a book and the dream of one day becoming a writer. Luckily, after a few failed career choices, she gets to follow that dream—writing down-to-earth contemporary romance and romantic suspense. From farmers to cowboys, Midwest to *the* West, Nicole writes stories about people finding themselves and finding love in the process. She lives in Missouri with her husband and two sons, and dreams of someday owning a barn.

Books by Nicole Helm

Harlequin Intrigue

Hudson Sibling Solutions

Cold Case Kidnapping
Cold Case Identity
Cold Case Investigation
Cold Case Scandal

Covert Cowboy Soldiers

The Lost Hart Triplet
Small Town Vanishing
One Night Standoff
Shot in the Dark
Casing the Copycat
Clandestine Baby

Visit the Author Profile page at Harlequin.com.

CAST OF CHARACTERS

Mary Hudson—Administrative assistant for Hudson Sibling Solutions and the organized glue that keeps the Hudson clan running.

Walker Daniels (aka Joe Beck, Steve Mier, Paul Anderson, etc.)—Oldest brother of the Daniels trio, on a lifelong mission to discover who killed his mother... without getting himself or his siblings killed first.

Chloe Brink—Mary's friend and a deputy at the Sunrise Sheriff's Department.

Anna Hudson-Steele—Mary's little sister, married to Hawk Steele, currently pregnant.

Carlyle and Zeke Daniels—Walker's siblings.

Jack Hudson—The oldest Hudson brother, sheriff of Sunrise and head of Hudson Sibling Solutions.

Palmer Hudson—Mary's brother and an investigator with HSS. Engaged to Louisa O'Brien.

Grant Hudson—Mary's brother, former military and current investigator with HSS, in a relationship with Dahlia Easton.

Cash Hudson—Mary's brother who trains dogs and lives in a cabin on the Hudson property. He has an eleven-year-old daughter, Izzy.

Chapter One

Mary Hudson was not like her siblings. They seemed to be determined to run toward danger, no matter the costs. Jack, her oldest brother, was the sheriff of tiny Sunrise, Wyoming. Grant had gone to war, though he'd thankfully returned. Cash, well, Cash had a daughter and had sworn off danger as much as he could, so maybe he and Mary were a little more alike than the others. Then there was Palmer, who'd played football and done a few years in the rodeo, and while he had settled down a bit the past year, he still took on dangerous cold case investigations as part of the family business.

And then there was Anna, who had been forced to slow down because of her current pregnancy, but Mary had no doubt her baby sister would be wreaking havoc once again when the baby was born. Though her husband, Hawk, would try to tame her, fool in love that he was.

Mary, on the other hand, had much preferred a life of order. Ever since her parents had disappeared when she was ten years old, she'd stepped in to be the structure sorely lacking in a household of five children being raised by their eighteen-year-old brother.

Oh, Jack was stern and strict and all those things, but he had nothing on Mary. Mary just knew how to wrap it up in a pleasant smile and soft words, and give people the impression she was biddable and sweet all the while she maneuvered them into exactly what she knew they needed.

At the end of the day, people were simple. Life was hard, violence and tragedy inevitable, but people themselves were easy.

So, she knew that instead of going to Jack with her request, she'd need to go to one of the other officers at Sunrise SD. Because Jack was by the book and tired of hearing her talk about this one administrative error.

Her four brothers—all older, hardheaded, obnoxious—seemed to think that it was perfectly acceptable for them to hold on to a client's deposit when the client had disappeared before they'd done any work for them.

Mary did not agree. Though she didn't do any of the cold case investigations with Hudson Sibling Solutions, she did everything else. Accounting, administration and a long list of other tasks it took to run a business, while her siblings did all the dangerous work.

So, Mary was the one who got to call the shots in this case. In her estimation, it was imperative they return the money to the client. If she had to be the one to track Mr. Joe Beck down and return his money to either him or, if he was no longer, one of his kin, then so be it.

It was only right and fair.

She currently sat at the small diner in Sunrise, waiting for Chloe Brink, both her friend *and* an officer with Sunrise SD. Because Chloe was not afraid of bending a few rules.

Mary was pretty sure her brother Jack would spontaneously combust at the mere thought.

Chloe came in wearing her Sunrise SD uniform—more casual than a lot of the police departments as it was just a polo with a badge and then pants of the officer's choosing. Chloe slid into the booth across from Mary, immediately reached across and swiped Mary's mug of coffee and took a big swig.

Mary wasn't sure why, but she tended to make friends with people who were not like her. She supposed it came from always running herd on her baby sister, who was brash, outspoken and, well, a pill. It took a strong personality to enjoy Anna, and so any person Mary might have enjoyed who was more reserved didn't stick around for long.

At least Mary knew what to do with brash, outspoken women.

"I ordered you one to go," Mary said primly.

Chloe only grinned. "Yeah, but I needed a jolt ASAP." She plopped a folder onto the table between them. "So, I did some digging into your guy. Looks like he's got some aliases."

"Oh." Mary frowned. Aliases seemed bad. "Criminal type aliases?"

"Not exactly—at least nothing concrete on any record I could find. But definitely someone who wants to stay under the radar. This is the last known address I have for Joe Beck," Chloe said, taking out a piece of paper from the folder. "It's over in Hardy."

Mary reached for the paper, but Chloe held her hand over it before Mary could fully pull it toward her.

"You're just going to send him like a check or something, right?" Chloe asked suspiciously.

"Who do you take me for?" Mary replied primly.

"A Hudson," Chloe replied with a laugh. "You might fancy yourself the calm, organized one who lets her siblings do all the wading in and causing trouble, but Mary Hudson, you *always* get your way."

Mary didn't bother arguing with it. It was true. She knew how to get her way, because more often than not, her way was correct.

The waitress appeared with the to-go cup of coffee and handed it to Chloe, who had to relinquish her hold on the paper.

Mary took it. An address in Hardy. She could take a drive out that way this morning and be back at the ranch before anyone really noticed. "Do you have a list of the aliases?"

Chloe passed over the whole file. "He's a bit of a mystery, Mary. You go poking around in it, it's possible you're wading in deeper than you want."

"I never wade in deeper than I want." Mary looked at the list. Joe Beck—the man she was looking for. Steve Mier. Paul Anderson. Well, it didn't matter what he went by, she'd get his money back to him.

"You just jinxed yourself," Chloe said, quite seriously for a cop who had to know *jinxing* had nothing to do with life.

"I don't believe in jinxes or curses or your rabbit's foot or the crystals you evangelize. I have also never once burned sage."

"Oh, no, you're really doing it."

Mary shook her head. "Go ahead, universe. Throw it all at me," she said, because she enjoyed the look of pain and amusement that crossed Chloe's face.

"Don't go trying to find this guy, Mary. That area of Hardy isn't the best, and I hate to break it to you, but I agree with Jack on this one."

Mary scowled. "You should really second-guess your life choices if you're agreeing with Jack."

"Trying to return money someone doesn't seem to want returned is a pointless exercise. Send the guy a letter. Send him a check, but don't go down there. Or if you simply *must*, since it's you and you will, don't go alone. Take one of your brothers, or I'll go with you on my next day off."

"I'm sure that won't be necessary."

"Oh, don't pull out the queen of the ranch voice on me,"

Chloe said, standing. She was frowning, but Mary knew it was out of concern.

Mary stood, too, and handed Chloe the to-go cup. "Don't forget your coffee."

Chloe's frown didn't change, but she sighed. "Be careful, Mary."

"I always am." And she was. She *was* the careful one. This wasn't reckless. This was seeing something through. It wasn't right to keep the money. She could hardly put *money for services not rendered* on their taxes, so she wouldn't keep it.

Mary left the diner and drove out of Sunrise, the pretty Western town surrounded by ranches—including her family's. Then to the larger town of Hardy that had more jobs to offer. She didn't call one of her brothers. She didn't ask someone to come along.

She could handle this on her own.

She may have had second thoughts as she pulled into a parking spot in the run-down apartment complex, but surely if the man lived *here*, he needed the money returned to him all that much more than she'd thought.

She was doing him a favor, and the right thing. That was all that mattered.

She got out of her car. People sat on porches eyeing her, or her car more likely. Maybe her purse. But she was not the little princess she might appear. She was tough. She had been shot. Actually shot last month. Maybe the bullet had just grazed her arm, but she was officially tough.

Or so she told herself as her insides shook with nerves. She moved forward, chin high and not bothering to make eye contact with anyone. She ignored comments and attempts to get her attention and walked up the stairs to the door listed on the address.

She knocked. She heard something inside, but no one

opened the door. She knocked again. "Mr. Beck?" she called, ignoring the creepy feeling she was being watched. "My name is…" Well, maybe she shouldn't be shouting her name around here. "I'm from Hudson Sibling Solutions. I wanted to—"

The door opened. A man stood there. He was dressed all in black, which matched his hair and maybe even his eyes, which were a dark, dark brown. He was tall and broad-shouldered, but rangy. Those dark eyes were direct and angry.

He had an old scar on his chin and a crooked nose, and it *shouldn't* have been appealing, especially when matched with the angry eyes, but she couldn't ignore the fact that he was startlingly handsome. Wild, sure, but handsome.

Not that she went for the wild sort, but—

With no warning, she was jerked inside and all she could think was: *well, darn.*

She had dared the universe, and now she was going to pay.

WALKER DANIELS DIDN'T have the first earthly clue who the pretty, primly dressed woman who came to his door was, but he'd recognized one of his aliases and figured ignoring her wouldn't work.

Especially here. Especially with what was coming.

"Who are you?" he demanded.

Her eyes were wide on the array of guns he had laid out on his table. He'd been packing up, getting ready to go. Someone had figured him out, and he knew it was too dangerous to stick around and find out who.

Though the *who* was the answer to everything, Walker was determined to stay alive first and foremost. If it meant another few years chasing down his mother's killer, he'd do it.

He'd do whatever it took to find answers, and to keep his sister and brother safe.

End of story.

"Are you Joe Beck?" she asked, and he'd give her credit. She might be a willowy thing, looking better suited to walk a runway than slum it here in this crappy apartment building, but she had backbone.

He paused for a second he didn't have. Joe Beck had been an old alias, but he couldn't remember ever dealing with this woman under any of his names.

He'd remember. He remembered faces. Besides, she was pretty. Always a pleasure to remember a pretty woman. But he couldn't place this one, so there was no way he'd met her.

"Come on, we've got to get you out of here." He moved for the guns, began to put them in his bag as she inched her way back toward the door. He'd let her go if she ran, but it'd be safer if he escorted her out.

Safer for *her*. Then again, maybe this strange woman would throw whoever was close off his scent. They'd be looking for one man, not a man and a woman.

Especially a woman who had legs like that and was wearing a billowy skirt that showed them off when she moved.

"Mr. Beck, I only need to refund you your money, and then I will be on my way." She pulled an envelope from her purse and handed it to him.

He stared at it. Was this some kind of trap? "What the hell are you talking about?" But he didn't give her a chance to answer because he got that feeling. The skin prickle at the back of his neck. That gut feeling that always kept him just one step ahead of the people who wanted him as dead as his mother.

He pulled the woman to the ground. He was about 90 percent sure she was an innocent bystander, so he'd protect her. But he'd also keep an eye on her because there was a

10 percent chance his gut was wrong. He covered her body with his.

She let out a little squeak of surprise from underneath him.

"I don't know who you are, lady, but you sure walked into the wrong apartment complex."

"My name is Mary Hudson," she said, as if she was sitting behind a desk, or maybe in the front of a classroom, giving a lecture. "I am with Hudson Sibling Solutions. Now, you're going to need to get off me."

He was barely listening to her, though he was surprised at how still she remained rather than try to fight him off. He didn't know if it was terror or sense that held her still, but right now it didn't matter.

The shots would come. He knew they would.

As if on cue, the window shattered at one side of the apartment. Which gave him enough information to know where they'd storm his apartment from.

Time for the escape route. He rolled off her but pulled her with him. "Keep low," he muttered, grabbing his bag from the table without standing up. She kept up. Clearly someone shooting his window out had not rendered her into the expected terrified mess.

He didn't have time to wonder why that was. He could only grab what he needed and pull her with him to the back of the apartment. His rear window looked out over an alley, and he'd had this escape route planned for a few days now.

He tossed the bags out onto the little cushion he'd made behind some random-looking boxes and other alley debris the trash truck wouldn't pick up. He unfurled the makeshift ladder he'd worked out how to attach to the windowsill so it could bear weight. They'd have to take it one at a time since he'd only tested it with his weight.

"You first," he said, motioning for the ladder.

She looked out the window, then down the side of the building, then back at him. She opened her mouth to say something—likely an argument, or maybe she'd try to shove some money at him again, as if *that* made sense. But there was no time.

"Better hurry," Walker urged. "They'll figure it out soon enough and come around back."

The woman firmed her mouth but listened, climbing down the rickety ladder. She definitely wasn't dressed for it, and Walker couldn't help but wish he were on the bottom of the ladder to catch the show, but as it was, he kept an eye on his front door.

Just as Mary took the last little jump onto the concrete below, a bullet crashed through the door.

Walker swung out and onto the ladder, going down as fast as he could, then jumping off the minute he was close enough to the ground not to break a leg. He gave the ladder a hard yank and it tumbled to the ground. He tossed it into the dumpster, then grabbed the woman's hand and pulled her down the alley toward his car.

Well, one of his cars. One that fit in in this side of town.

She tugged her hand out from his grasp and stood next to the car. He kept expecting her to break into fear or panic, but she was filled with nothing but a cool kind of skepticism as she looked at his car. "I don't believe I should go with you."

"Maybe you'd like to go with the guys shooting at me instead?"

"Well, no."

"Then get the hell in," Walker said, sliding into the driver's seat. He tossed his bags in the back—except one gun he put in the middle console for easy reach. The way he saw it, they had a minute, tops, before the bullets started again. "This car leaves in three seconds," he told her before closing his door.

He thought she'd hesitate longer than three, but she was

in the passenger side—and buckled of all things—in two. She clearly wasn't pleased, but she still didn't look scared. Walker shook his head, reminding himself that he'd have time to figure that out later. "Keep low," he instructed. "They're going to follow. Hold on."

Chapter Two

Mary understood danger better than most, so she'd gone ahead and gotten in the car with the man. She knew how to pick the lesser of two evils.

But she was considering all her escape options as the man—clearly *not* Joe Beck—drove like a lunatic through the, thankfully, rather empty streets of Hardy.

"Do you know where you're going?"

The man did not look at her, which was good since he was currently conducting an illegal U-turn, then screeching into a turn down a one-way street.

The wrong way.

Mary wanted to close her eyes, but instead she kept her gaze steady on the driver. The man was likely to get her killed before he even took her wherever he was taking her. Which was also, likely, her eventual death.

"Yeah, I know." He turned again, this time onto a two-way road that allowed Mary to breathe a little easier. He zoomed onto the highway, headed west. Mary wondered how long he'd go. She tried to get a glimpse at the gas gauge, but the dashboard was so dusty she didn't think even *he* could see it.

He slowed his pace now. Drove more like a normal person who cared at all about safety. Even his posture relaxed, and he flicked a glance her way.

"You're a cool one, aren't you?"

She clutched her hands a little tighter, lifted her chin. Because *cool* was about all the defense she had against fear, and fear had been a rather constant companion since she'd been ten years old.

So, she had her coping mechanisms, and if that was *cool*, so be it. What did she care what this mysterious, dangerous stranger thought anyway?

"Where are you taking me?" Mary asked, keeping her tone prim and *cool*.

"I've got a few places. The one outside Sunrise is probably the best option for this."

"Sunrise," she repeated. Close to home. Close enough she might be able to *get* home.

"Don't worry, I'll get you back to wherever you came from eventually," he continued. "Just got to make sure the coast is clear first."

Mary tried to wrap her mind around what he was saying. That he didn't plan on hurting her. Of course, a criminal didn't tend to announce his intentions to his victims.

"Who *are* you?"

He flashed a grin in her direction. "I've gone by Joe Beck, and a few other names."

"Steve Mier. Paul Anderson." She thought she maybe saw a flash of surprise that she knew his other aliases, but only a flash, if that.

"You can call me any of those," he said with a shrug.

"But what's your *real* name?"

He paused. She wasn't sure she expected the truth out of a man who'd just…whatever they'd just done. Certainly she shouldn't find a man with a bag of guns and planned escape routes from his apartment trustworthy.

"Not important really," he said at long last.

Mary sighed and looked at the world around them. They would pass right by the Hudson Ranch. She eyed his profile. Her gut hadn't told her to jump out of the moving car just yet. Besides, if anyone could handle themselves against one man with guns, it was her family. She pointed to the turnoff up ahead.

"Turn up there."

He eyed her then, suspiciously. "Why?"

"Because that's where I live. We can figure out this money situation, and you'll have a decent place to hide for a bit. The ranch is huge. We may even be able to help you. Depending."

"Depending on what?"

"On whether you're on the right side of the law."

"The right side of the law." He snorted derisively, but he turned at the road. "I don't have much concern about the law."

"Well, that might be a problem as my brother is the sheriff of Sunrise."

The car began to slow, but Mary reached over and put her hand on his arm, pointing ahead.

"Don't stop. Go on up and around the house to the back. Jack won't be here. You helped me, in a way, I guess. If you really need to get out of here before he comes, I'll be sure you do. But we need to sort out this Joe Beck money."

He eyed her. She thought he was coming to the same sort of conclusion she had come to. Certainly they couldn't trust each other, but gut feelings didn't lie. And *she* wasn't bad or a liar. She didn't think he was…bad precisely.

Besides, with everything that had happened in her life—from her parents' disappearance, to the past few months of repeated and constant danger for her siblings—it was easy enough to take this in stride.

She dealt with cold cases as a matter of course. Weird was the name of the game. And learning to trust your gut was just part of the process.

He looked down at her hand on his arm, and though she told herself not to react, she jerked her hand back anyway. A bit like she'd been burned. Embarrassment fought its way up her face.

She didn't even know why she was embarrassed.

Except maybe because she'd noticed his arms were very impressive.

She wanted to close her eyes in shame, but instead she turned her gaze to the house.

He let out a low whistle as his dark eyes surveyed the world around them—all Hudson land, for a good century or so. "Should I be calling you Princess?" he asked, turning his attention to her.

She lifted her chin. "I prefer Queen, thank you."

He grinned at her, and she felt a strange little flutter deep in her chest. And the strange desire to smile right back, when honestly his smile was predatory. At best.

"Park around back, Mr. Beck. And we'll get this all sorted," Mary said, hoping she sounded as contained as she usually did.

He shook his head, though he did keep driving the car around the back. "You know what? I changed my mind." He parked, even got out of the car, and she had to scurry after him.

"Changed your mind about what?" she asked, suddenly wondering if she'd made a terrible mistake trusting her gut.

"I don't like the way you say *Mr. Beck*. Call me Walker. That's my real name." And then he strode toward the back door, like this was *his* house. Like *he* was in charge.

And no, that would not do.

NONE OF THIS made a heap of sense to Walker, but this big old house wouldn't be a hardship to hide away at. He didn't love the whole brother-sheriff thing, and thought maybe she was tricking him into some kind of citizen's arrest.

But a man didn't survive years chasing his mother's killer to get caught quite so easily—whether by shooters or sheriffs.

Mary stalked in front of him, clearly trying to keep a handle on her temper because even though her strides were brisk, her expression was perfectly calm on her very beautiful face. He wondered if she tried to look a little plain, a little severe on purpose.

But it didn't quite work, because her hair was mussed from everything that had happened back at his apartment, and her color was a little high. Admirable control, but someone didn't have admirable control unless there was a tempest of responses underneath it all.

A tempting thought, that. He knew, even knowing next to nothing about her, she was as far out of his league as this house was, but that didn't mean he didn't enjoy the view.

She opened the door, held it for him with the understanding he'd follow her inside.

"Thanks, Your Highness."

He watched her face get a little pinched and tried not to laugh. "Sorry, what did you say your name was again?"

My name is Mary Hudson. I am with Hudson Sibling Solutions. Now, you're going to need to get off me. She'd said that very calmly back in his apartment, and Walker didn't forget much. But he found it best to pretend like he wasn't paying attention. Let people think he was forgetful or concerned with other things.

Underestimating him always worked in his favor.

"My name is Mary Hudson," she said, and it seemed a bit like she spoke between gritted teeth. But then she smiled blandly at him and gestured him inside.

This back door led into a kind of mudroom, filled with

all sorts of coats and boots. It was a big house, so he supposed it made sense it was full of a big family.

But he'd already checked out her hand and she didn't wear any rings. Even if she worked the ranch and kept things more subtle, she was definitely not the kind of woman who didn't wear a ring if she was married.

He followed her deeper into the house, into what appeared to be a dining room, where a woman paced the length of a very long table, muttering darkly into the phone at her ear. "I'm going to skin you alive, I hope you know."

Mary seemed wholly unfazed by this threat. "She must be speaking to her husband," she whispered. "That's my sister. Anna."

Walker winged up an eyebrow at that, but the woman pulled the phone away from her ear and shoved it into her pocket. Behind pretty hazel eyes, she studied him as if filing all the ways he might be a threat.

The sisters didn't look too much alike. This one was a little shorter, a little curvier. Blonde and fairer than Mary. They didn't even hold themselves the same. This woman looked like a brawler, even with the little hint of a baby bump.

"Anna," Mary said in her prim way. "This is Mr. Beck."

The woman's eyes registered surprise, and she studied him once more with this new information. "So, you finally tracked the ghost down. I don't know why I'm surprised."

"The ghost?" Walker looked at Mary.

"It's been almost a year since we received a down payment for a case we never were given the details about. Which left us unable to actually investigate. I've been trying to refund the money ever since, but by then Joe Beck seemingly disappeared."

Yeah, into Paul Anderson when his Joe Beck identity had gotten a little too easy to track. But that didn't explain *this*, because he had certainly never contacted anyone about an investigation or paid anyone. "What do you mean *case* and *investigate*?"

"Hudson Sibling Solutions," Anna supplied, as if those words might mean something to him.

He shrugged. "Never heard of it."

The sisters frowned at each other.

"You bring home the wrong Joe Beck, Mary?"

"No, I most certainly did not," Mary replied, and it was clear the more prim she sounded the more pissed she was. "Perhaps you don't remember because it was so long ago. Hudson Sibling Solutions investigates cold cases. We have a staff of trained private investigators skilled and experienced to get to the bottom of cases law enforcement can't give the necessary effort toward any longer."

She sounded like a brochure, and he had better things to do with his day. Or so he told himself as it was no hardship watching her talk.

But he shrugged, looked from Mary to Anna. "I don't have the first clue what you're talking about."

There was a tiny crack in Mary's calm facade. Her eyebrows lowered, though her mouth was still arranged in that polite little smile.

"Okay, what about this? Do you have any cold cases in your life, Joe?"

He didn't scowl, though he desperately wanted to. Something about these Hudson women and the way they said his fake name really scraped at him, like nails on a chalkboard.

And like hell he was going to bring up his cold case. Because he didn't need help, had never once asked for or hired help. And never would.

"Look, I didn't pay you this money. I didn't hire any Hudson Sibling Solutions. Maybe it was some other Joe Beck, because I can handle my own..."

Anna smirked, because it was enough to confirm that yes, he did have a cold case. This time Walker did scowl. He didn't have to stay here. He didn't have to deal with these two. His car was right out back, and no doubt there'd been just enough time that he'd lost whoever was shooting at him.

The plan had been to go hide out at the shack he had outside Sunrise, but unfortunately that was connected to the fake Joe Beck, and with them bandying about the name, it'd be better if he went back to his Paul Anderson identity.

Which finally made him think about what Mary had said. A year ago. A cold case. Joe Beck.

Damn it. Carlyle. "Hold on. Let me make a phone call." Because if this was true, his sister had some explaining to do.

Chapter Three

Mary could *feel* her sister studying her. So she went about tidying the dining room while Walker stepped outside to make his phone call. She expressly ignored Anna's study.

"Soooo…" Anna said after a few seconds, because that was all her impetuous sister was capable of staying silent for.

"So?" Mary went around the table, straightening all the chairs so they looked the way she preferred.

"He looks…wild."

He did indeed look wild, and Mary was no fan of wild. She liked order. Hence the chairs. "If you say so."

"And *you*, Mary Hudson, came in looking disheveled."

Mary stopped what she was doing, because the insinuation Anna was making was so beyond ludicrous even she couldn't pretend. She glared at her sister. "What are you suggesting?"

"I'm *wishing* you got hot and heavy with the attractive outlaw-looking gentleman who may or may not be our Joe Beck ghost, but I'm *suggesting* it's something much more boring. I want to know what."

"It wasn't boring," Mary said with a sniff. Then regretted it, because she really didn't need any of her siblings knowing she'd thrown herself into all the trouble they'd warned her against. "He's in trouble."

Anna huffed out a breath. "Oh, Mary. Don't go collecting strays."

"I'm not collecting strays. I accidentally stepped into the middle of some of his danger, and since he was…" She couldn't say *kind enough*. She didn't think it had anything to do with kindness. "Since he didn't leave me to get caught in the middle and fend for myself, I offered him a place to hide out while he sorts through what needs sorting."

"Did you bother to check if he was on the right side of all this trouble?"

"When has that mattered to you, Anna?" Mary returned, wondering if she had time to vacuum the rug before Walker came back in.

"Touché," Anna replied with a grin. "But it matters to you, and it'll hardcore matter to Jack."

At their older brother's name, Mary turned her gaze back to Anna. "About that."

Anna's eyebrows winged up. "You're going to keep a secret from Jack?"

"I'm a grown woman. And it's not a secret. We just aren't going to mention it because it's not going to matter."

"Awfully high on our royal *we* horse."

Mary took a careful, calming breath. "I know you'll keep it from Jack because there's no point discussing it with him. I'm going to get Mr. Beck to take the money, and then he'll likely go on his way." She glanced at the door where he'd walked out. She wondered if he was taking off as they spoke.

None of her business, of course, but… She couldn't help but wonder what he was running from.

"Anna, I'd like you to look into this." She looked at Anna. "Without anyone knowing. It's delicate, I think. But he might be in trouble, and we could possibly help. If you need to tell Hawk, I understand, but—"

"That won't be necessary."

At the sound of the deep male voice, both women turned to find Walker standing in the doorway. Mary inwardly cursed herself for speaking so freely knowing he was around, but she'd half expected him to already be gone. She also understood he'd reentered the house silently on purpose.

"I don't need you interfering in what's already a delicate business. I am a grown man, and I've been dealing with this for over a decade. So just…leave it."

Mary felt her heart pinch at how closed off he seemed. Angry. Like something had changed. "Mr. Beck—"

"I told you, it's *Walker*," he snapped.

"And Beck isn't your real last name."

"You're damn right it ain't. And if you think I'm about to tell you what it is, you're out of your mind. Now, I'll be going. But I'll take that money, because apparently, it's my sister's. She used my name with some insane idea to… Well, it doesn't matter. I'll be taking it." He held out his hand, anger pumping off him.

Interesting he'd be angry now, when back at his apartment with people shooting at him he'd seemed…not happy about it, of course, but very comfortable and resigned to whatever danger he was in.

Maybe wanting to stop him from leaving came from her penchant for wanting to help. Anna called it *taking in strays*, but Mary considered it the very human need to want to make someone else comfortable.

"Over a decade is a long time, Walker," Mary returned calmly. She pulled the envelope from her purse once more. "We specialize in cold cases. Whatever it is you're searching for, it's possible we could help."

"I don't want or need help."

"That's too bad." She held the envelope out to him, and

he snatched it out of her hands before turning on a heel and leaving out the door again.

Mary watched him go, resisting the urge to follow. He'd made it clear he didn't want her help, and she tried not to be like her family of steamrollers, but… He clearly *did* need help if he was running from gunmen. Which, of course, didn't mean he was a good person or doing the right thing. She knew this.

Logically.

She also tended to trust her judgment of people. She'd always had an inherent ability to understand when someone was in trouble. Okay, so her therapist in college had said it was a trauma response to losing her parents so tragically at ten, and that she'd learned how to read a room and a person from there. Sought to fix other people's problems as a way of not dealing with her own.

Mary preferred to think of it as a useful skill.

"Go on after him," Anna said a few seconds after Walker had disappeared. "You know you want to. You can never resist an injured bird. Even if it's a criminal bird."

Mary knew she was supposed to laugh, but there was something about the man… A familiar kind of desperation she understood all too well. Even without bullets flying. "I don't think he's a criminal."

"No, I don't think so either. But we better make sure about it. I'll do that. You go on after him. Stay where the cameras can see you."

Mary nodded. Due to all the danger over the past few months, they had an extensive video surveillance system, so Anna would be able to keep an eye on her in case Walker did turn out to be more of a criminal than a man on a mission.

And hopefully nothing out of the ordinary happened today so Jack didn't feel the need to look through the footage.

Mary stepped outside, surprised to find Walker had

stopped himself. He stood next to his car, though he had his driver's side door open. He was looking out over the mountains. When she came closer, he turned his dark gaze to her.

"You've got a hell of a view," he muttered.

"Yes, we do," she agreed pleasantly, though her heart had begun to drum oddly in her chest when his eyes met hers. She swallowed down that strange, foreign feeling and forced herself to make the offer.

"You've made it clear you don't want Hudson Sibling Solutions' help, and I won't belabor the point except to point out we have almost fifteen years' experience, and while our track record isn't perfect, our success rate is high. We have a lot of different services to offer, and if there's something that's been going on in your life for an entire decade, we would be an asset."

"Yeah, you're really not belaboring the point."

She ignored him, and his focused gaze. "All that being said, this is a big ranch. If you need a place to stay for a while, to hide, I can accommodate you. Even if you don't want our help."

He looked down at her skeptically. "What about this sheriff brother of yours?"

"Like I said, it's a big ranch. He doesn't have to know. If you're careful."

"I'm always careful."

"I highly doubt that," she said with a sniff.

Which seemed to cause his mouth to curve. "What about your sister?"

"She'll keep it on the down-low. Anna lives to keep things on the down-low. Particularly from Jack."

"Why?"

"She's contrary?"

"No, why are you trying to help me?"

Mary sucked in a breath and looked around the ranch,

her home. It should be a safe place, but her parents had disappeared out there. Danger had come for her siblings, time and time again. And she'd always had someone to step in and help. Help didn't magically solve every problem, but it sure eased things.

"Sometimes you have to be the help you wished you'd had."

"That's stupid."

She wanted to scowl but didn't let herself. "Only if you're unarmed and unprepared." She turned her best officious smile on him. "We're always prepared, and *very* armed."

He chuckled at that, then shook his head as if he couldn't believe what he was saying. "I guess if you've got a place I could lay low at for tonight, I wouldn't say no."

WALKER WAS WELL aware of the risks he was taking as he drove Mary to the stables as she instructed. She insisted his car wouldn't make it to the place she had in mind, so she was going to lead him by horse until the car was hidden away, then he'd either have to walk the rest of the way or hop on the horse with her.

Walker waited in his car while she disappeared into the stable. He was sure he was walking himself into more trouble than he could afford, but something about Mary Hudson was compelling enough, he couldn't seem to resist.

It wasn't a strange sensation, exactly. He tended to skirt the line of danger in his quest to get answers, tended to make some rash or spontaneous decisions simply because they *felt* right.

But he'd never had it come in such a pretty package before.

She emerged from the stables with a horse, and she swung up on the huge animal in a mesmerizing move of grace and a flash of leg, since she was still wearing that floaty skirt.

She motioned for him to follow, and he found himself doing so without even questioning it. It was clear she loved horse riding. The land. Walker felt compelled to understand that, follow that.

She led him along a gravel road that got less and less gravel and more mud the farther they got, moving away from all the buildings and closer to mountains and cows.

She came to a stop, motioned for him to do the same and pointed to a little patch of dirt behind some scrubby bushes and scraggly trees.

He pushed the car into Park, turned off the ignition and got out. "This pasture isn't going to be used this year," she said to him, from where she sat high on the horse. "A little bit more of a walk and there's a cabin you can stay in for a spell. You can either walk, or you can climb on." She patted the back of her saddle.

He eyed her, the horse and said saddle and briefly wondered if she was insane. "I'll walk."

She cocked her head, still staring down at him. "Afraid?" she asked, and amusement curved her lips into an alluring smile.

Walker had grown up hopping from city to city, in what as a kid he'd thought was his mom's wanderlust. Once she'd been murdered, he realized she'd been running. All those years, running and making them think it was a grand adventure.

But he was a city boy, even if his investigations had brought him to the wilds of Bonesteel, South Dakota, or Bent County, Wyoming. He didn't trust horses, or any animal that could crush him. It was hardly fear.

But he figured any way he denied the question would only make him sound afraid. So he shrugged. "If you say so."

She didn't belabor the point, just made a noise and the

horse started trotting, slower than before when he'd been following by car.

They came around a little cluster of trees eventually and Walker stopped. He'd been expecting some kind of lean-to shack. Like what he had outside Sunrise. Sure, this ranch spread was nice as all get out, but he didn't think that extended to the far reaches of a not-used pasture.

But the cabin looked to be in pristine condition. It was small, sure, but it wasn't anywhere near shabby or falling apart. He forced himself to finish walking and met Mary at the front porch as she swung off her horse.

"One of our ranch hands lived here a while ago. We haven't hired a full-time replacement, so there won't be any reason for anyone to be coming out this way. The electricity's been turned off, but you've got water, a bed. You shouldn't start a fire to cook anything, so I'll bring you some food out in a bit."

She pulled a little key chain out of her pocket and twisted a key off the ring. "This'll get you in. I know you've got quite a few weapons, so you'll want to lock up just in case. You just leave the key behind on the kitchen counter when you go for good, and that's how I'll know to stop bringing you food. How's that?" She looked up at him, dark eyes squinting against the now-high sun.

"You're letting me stay here. For an undetermined amount of time. You're going to feed me. All because…"

"Well, the way I see it, you could have left me back there to get shot at. So, one kindness deserves another."

He hadn't had a whole lot of good in his life. The world had been cruel and unfair, and he'd figured that was fine. He could deal, try to protect his brother and sister from that. In the end, protecting them was all that had ever really mattered to him as an adult.

Mary handed him the key, and he took it. But he didn't

go inside. He narrowed his eyes at her, wondering who let her wander around so naive and trusting. "I could be a dangerous criminal. You know that, right?"

"Of course."

"I could kill you. Right here. Tie you up in there and torture you, if I had a mind."

She didn't flinch, didn't back away, just held his gaze with that steady coolness that shouldn't irritate him as much as it did.

"If you had a mind. But you don't. Or you would have already done any of those things." She lifted that chin, all regal and dismissive. "I'm not afraid of you."

"Maybe you should be." He wanted her to be, so she'd keep her distance. Stop making his thoughts drift to strange places he didn't recognize within himself. Like someone who believed she might really be helping him out of the goodness of her heart.

"You have a sister, you said. Is she younger?"

He frowned at the change in conversation but nodded. He probably shouldn't have mentioned Carlyle, but it was what it was. She *had* been the one to hire HSS anyway. Luckily it sounded like Zeke had been as in the dark as Walker, so only one of his siblings was a traitor.

"And you've likely protected her for some portion of her life?" Mary continued with that lady-of-the-manor chin lift.

He frowned deeper and didn't bother to agree even though, yeah, he'd protected her for more than a portion of her life.

"So you should understand I have four older brothers. One's a sheriff, as I mentioned. One is a former marine. If you tried to harm me in any way, I can guarantee, no matter how tough you think you are, they would hurt you right back. And worse, especially when all four of them get together. They can be very unreasonable when provoked."

"That so?"

"And then, worst of all, there's Anna."

"The tiny pregnant woman?"

"She'd flat out kill you, Walker. Without batting an eye. And her husband would help her bury your body, no doubt. With a smile on his face. He's very devoted."

He wanted to laugh—not because he didn't believe her, but because he just couldn't quite peg her, when he usually had everyone down within seconds of meeting them. Like her sister, for example, whom he fully believed would kill him if given the chance.

"What about you? You're not dangerous?" he asked, wondering how she fit into the little tableau she'd painted.

"I'm whatever I need to be. Now, you go on and settle in. I'll be back later with some dinner." And before he could refuse, she was easily mounting the horse and trotting away. A woman on a mission.

He watched her go, enjoying the view and wondering if he was the naive one, believing in a pretty face just because it came in a nicely dressed package that didn't seem to blink at oncoming danger.

And danger was coming, whether he stayed or left.

Chapter Four

Mary went through dinner as if she was not harboring a potential fugitive from the law in their currently unoccupied ranch hand cabin. She made the meal while her brother Cash and his daughter, Izzy, took their turn setting the table. She sat with her family and discussed the ranch and HSS business all the while eating the dinner she'd prepared.

She was quite sure no one suspected anything—she was quite adept at keeping things to herself—but every time she glanced at Anna, she felt guilty. After dinner, Palmer and Cash pretended to argue over whose turn it was to do the dishes, which made Izzy grin and was likely why they did it.

Mary made herself scarce as she often did this time of night. She couldn't keep up with all the chores if she handled them herself, but if she couldn't have them done her way, she could *not* be witness to the incorrect loading of the dishwasher or putting leftovers away.

She might be a control freak, but she could delegate. As long as she didn't have to bear witness.

So, she went to her room for a few hours and caught up on the necessary paperwork for both the ranch and HSS. Anna popped in about halfway through her work. "Couldn't find anything bad on him. Doesn't mean it isn't there. I couldn't find a Walker who connected to any of the aliases, but if he's got aliases, he's hiding something."

Mary agreed, but for some reason that just didn't change what she felt like she needed to do.

"Thank you."

"No problem." Anna settled herself on Mary's bed, clearly wanting to say more, but holding back.

"Did you have something else you wanted to discuss?" Mary asked, in the prim voice that usually irritated Anna.

On cue, Anna scowled at her. "Look, I'm not going to lecture you on being careful. I happen to think you should do at least one un-careful thing in your life. But I don't want to see you hurt." Anna's gaze dropped to Mary's arm, where she'd been shot last month when someone had tried to hurt the family.

But that had been about protecting her family. Not flinging herself into danger. "I know how to look after myself, Anna."

"Yes, I know you think you do. But sometimes…" She swept a hand down her body, her little baby bump. "A handsome man can create unintended consequences."

Mary laughed. "Anna, you can't be serious."

"He's good-looking. A little wounded animal—which is your personal kryptonite. I just want you to be careful-ish. Like, have some great, protected sex with a handsome, charming stranger. Be wild, but not too wild. Like not dodging bullets or getting kidnapped wild."

"So not *your* brand of wild?"

"Mary."

"I have no intention of getting caught up in whatever danger Walker has going on. I just offered him a place to lay low for a brief period of time. No doubt he'll be on his way tomorrow, to do whatever he needs to do."

Anna sighed. "If you say so."

When Mary didn't take the bait and argue, Anna left. Likely to go check on her husband, who was still recovering from his serious gunshot wound he'd gotten the same day Mary had gotten her minor one.

She studied the mark on her arm. Nothing more than a mostly healed scar. She couldn't say she'd handled any of that moment well, but she'd decided to move forward thinking of it as a badge of honor.

It was much better than thinking about how close Hawk had been to dying, or Anna had been to getting killed, or Cash and Izzy...

No. She wouldn't go down that road again. It was over. Done. They'd survived.

When it sounded like the house was still, she crept back down to the kitchen. She packed up some leftovers for Walker, sticking to things that would taste good cold or room temperature. She packed them in a cooler. He'd likely leave in the morning, but if he didn't, she wanted him to have enough food to get by on.

A handsome man can create unintended consequences.

Well, he was indeed a handsome man, but Mary was a controlled, careful woman. There were no unintended consequences in her future. God knew Walker had more pressing things on his mind than an uptight administrator of her family's businesses.

She frowned at her own description of herself. She liked her life. If she didn't, she'd change it. She didn't want excitement or what Anna called being *un-careful*. What happened this morning was the most excitement she needed, thank you very much.

But, in fairness, Anna was right about wounded animals. Mary couldn't resist trying to help. So, she crept out of the kitchen and to the back door. For a moment she paused and listened, just to make sure everyone was still and quiet where they were supposed to be.

Grant cozied up with his girlfriend, Dahlia, in his room.

Louisa and Palmer in theirs, an arrangement that wouldn't change until after their wedding when Palmer finished building a place on his stretch of land. Cash and Izzy lived in a cabin across the yard with their menagerie of dogs that Cash trained. Hawk and Anna were still in the house with their ever-growing puppy, but Pita slept in their room with them. They were talking about building, too, but Mary secretly hoped they stayed until after the baby was born.

Mary loved babies. She enjoyed Izzy at eleven just as much as she'd enjoyed the girl as an infant, but there was something about snuggly little babies that just turned Mary into goo. She supposed it helped she was an aunt not a mom, so didn't have to be plagued with pregnancy sickness or sleepless nights.

But tonight she wasn't worried about that, or her paired-up siblings. She was worried about Jack—the only person who didn't have someone claiming most of their evening attention. Well, the only one besides her.

Jack would likely be up. Poring over a case for work or checking up on HSS business. Would he hear the door open and close and come snooping? She frowned a little, because it struck her as sad, and she didn't want to feel pity for Jack when she was trying to commit a little subterfuge against him.

He would most definitely not approve of Walker in any sense. At least not until he had him fully checked out to make sure he wasn't a criminal. And since Anna hadn't been able to figure that out for sure, Jack would not approve.

It was only one night. A little help. And if she was aiding and abetting a criminal? Well, she supposed it'd be a mistake she'd learn from.

Careful, with all the stealth of a criminal, she slid out the back door and walked with calm purpose to the stables.

She saddled Pippi, settled the soft cooler in a saddlebag, then set off.

Mary loved riding. It was one of the few things she remembered doing with her parents that didn't bring the pain of grief. There was too much joy here, in the wind whipping through her hair. In the moon glowing high above the mountains.

Or maybe she didn't miss them here because she *felt* them. In the wind, in the moonlight. It was one of the few fanciful thoughts she allowed herself.

As she approached the cabin, it was shrouded in darkness, though if a person really looked they might notice the slight glow coming from the gap in the curtains.

She pulled Pippi to a stop, loosely tied her reins around the porch post, then went up to the door and knocked.

Walker opened the door. The inside was illuminated by a battery-powered lamp the previous tenant must have left behind. She slid inside, though this side of the ranch should be isolated enough not to have people seeing anything.

She held out the cooler. "Here you are, as promised. There's some food. I didn't pack any water since the sink water should be potable."

He unzipped the top, peered in. "This is quite the feast."

"It'll hopefully keep you going through tomorrow."

He opened one of the containers, gave the food a little sniff, then grabbed a bite. He nodded as he chewed. "Good."

He was clearly hungry. He made it through one container without saying anything else. Mary knew she should go, leave him to it. But she just stood there.

"So. What did the fam find out about me?" Walker asked, handing her the empty container so she could take it back with her.

"Nothing."

He raised an eyebrow. "You're telling me they didn't look into anything about me?"

"Oh, Anna looked. Well, she looked for a criminal record associated with any of your names."

"Yeah, don't have one of those."

"Because   it was the middle of the night and she was alone in this cabin with a stranger.

A very handsome stranger.

"Either that," he agreed easily, "or I just don't get caught."

WALKER WAS FASCINATED by the way Mary's expressions changed. Or didn't, as the case might be. She wore that coolness like a mask. A cloak of *I am not affected by you.*

Which meant he wondered, when she was looking down her nose at him and firmed her lips like that, if she was in fact *quite* affected.

And you do not have the time to care either way.

A fair reminder.

She didn't immediately leave, though she hovered there by the door. He was too hungry to care if she was watching him eat. He'd been busy with preparations this morning and hadn't had a chance to eat breakfast, then there'd been the shooting and Mary and the Hudson Ranch.

He could have gone foraging earlier—he'd made sure a long time ago he could survive any situation—but he'd trusted her to bring him food. That trust bothered him a little bit, but here she was. Watching him with those serious brown eyes.

"Did you want some?" he asked.

She shook her head. "I was just curious. What did your sister want us to investigate?"

The question surprised him when it shouldn't have. He'd already read Carlyle the riot act for involving other people, for using one of his fake names. But yelling at Carlyle never did anything.

So he wasn't sure why he still engaged. Something about his baby sister brought it out in him, he supposed.

He studied the woman asking the question, not afraid to let the silence stretch out. She didn't seem to be either. She just stood there, with a patient, steady stare, reminding him of the social worker he'd had to deal with when he'd wanted custody of Carlyle.

Not a bad person, not an enemy or a threat, and yet just like then, Walker kind of wanted to make her one.

He didn't like that reaction at all. He didn't mind the truth. The problem was it came with a hell of a lot of danger, and Mary... Well, she wasn't the kind of woman who was equipped to deal with danger, no matter what her family did.

"You planning on sticking around watching me eat or what?"

"I can go, if you'd rather."

He couldn't help but scowl at that placid nonanswer. "I'll probably be out of here by tomorrow afternoon. Once I'm sure they've stopped sniffing around Bent County."

"All right. Well, if you need to stay longer, know that you're more than welcome. I'll come by tomorrow evening around the same time with more food. If you're still here, it's yours. If not, no harm done." She smiled. Kindly.

And he didn't know what the hell to do with her kindness. He couldn't even muster his usual skepticism. She was just too...something.

She turned to leave and that seemed wrong. "My mother was murdered." What the hell was wrong with him? "Ten years ago."

She turned back to face him, her expression not shocked or pitying like the usual looks he got. She crossed the way and put her hand on his arm. "Oh, Walker. I'm so sorry."

She seemed so genuinely distressed for him. Not the usual pity, which came with either skepticism or a distancing of not knowing what to do with that information. Just a genuine expression of sympathy.

"And your father?" she asked gently, like she knew. When she didn't know a damn thing, in her prissy outfits on this sprawling ranch with her own damn horse.

"Mom ditched him when my baby sister was born. Fine enough to knock us around since we were boys, but once the girl came along it was time to do what she could." He didn't know where that came from, so bitter. So ugly. He knew his mother had tried her best.

Unfortunately, sometimes people's best wasn't good enough.

"You have a brother too?"

"Going to collect all this information, put it in some little database?" he returned, scowling down at her.

"I don't even know your last name, Walker," she said calmly, not at all put off by the snap in his tone. "My family could likely find it if they dug hard and long enough, but we won't poke if you don't want us to. But I hope you understand, we could help you. It's what we do. Because we've been through it."

He snorted. "Yeah? How?"

"My parents disappeared when I was ten years old. No one ever could figure out what happened to them. They were good, loving parents. But they just…" She swallowed. "They were gone. No hints. No evidence. If I believed in aliens, that would make sense, but I don't. So it's just this unsolved mystery."

Walker didn't know what to say, and that was a weird sensation. He'd been a fast talker in all situations as long as he could remember. He'd talked dear old dad around so he didn't start punching, sweet-talked his mom into letting him do something dumb, then the social workers, the teachers, then every person he'd had to work around to try to get to the bottom of what his mother had been running from.

What had caught up with her.

But he did not know what to say to Mary Hudson. The woman looked like she had it all but she'd lost her parents mysteriously at ten. Younger than Carlyle had been when Mom had died.

"We don't take our cold cases lightly, is my point," she said, when he didn't speak. "And you don't have to make the decision now. Anytime you want or need our help, we'll be happy to supply it."

"For a price?"

"Would you rather it be charity?" she returned archly.

He found himself wanting to laugh of all things. Who the hell *was* this woman? "So what happened? After your parents? You live with your grandparents or something?"

She shook her head. "Jack, my oldest sibling, he was eighteen. He fought tooth and nail to keep us and keep us together. And he did. While he was doing that, he also figured we might as well try to help people like us. Because we never got answers, and it'd be nice if someone did."

"I'm close enough to the answers all on my own," he returned, more out of reflex than anything else. How could he bring in outside help when someone wanted him and his siblings dead?

Mary didn't react to that, except to nod. "I guess I should go then."

But he had the bizarre and deep-seated urge to keep her here. "I don't really know what to do with help. I sure as hell don't know how to believe in the goodness of anyone's heart."

"Then *I'm* sorry, Walker. That sounds sad."

Maybe it was. But Mary needed to understand. "It's dangerous. Whoever killed her? They're trying to kill me so I don't find out who they are."

"You must be close then," she returned as if potential murders were just a matter of course. "We know what to do with danger. You know, I was shot last month."

Walker was tempted to laugh. "Shot, huh?"

She moved closer, pulled up her sleeve, and there was indeed a red little mark, clearly healing. He narrowed his eyes at her. "That's a graze."

"Done by a bullet."

"How?"

"Well, someone had set a fire at my brother's cabin. He and his daughter were trapped inside, so I ran outside to get to them, but someone was waiting and shot me. It was this whole thing about getting back at us for not finding a previous client's son before he died."

"Sounds pretty far-fetched."

"If you think *that's* far-fetched, I won't even tell you about my other brother uncovering a human-sacrificing cult a few months before that."

"You sound like bad luck, sweetheart."

She smiled at that when he thought she'd balk at him calling her sweetheart. In fact, he kept expecting her to balk—from that very first moment in his crappy apartment in Hardy to this one.

And she never did.

A moment of silence stretched out, and maybe he was staring a little too intently trying to figure her out. Or maybe it was just that she was a pretty little thing and he was a man with an impressive imagination, but a little pink seemed to creep into her cheeks and she took a step back toward the door.

"Well, I should go back to the house. Just understand, like this cabin, help is an open offer."

"All right."

She slid back out the door as carefully as she'd entered, and Walker knew he shouldn't. But like everything with Mary, knowing better didn't seem to change his actions. He moved over to the window, looked out the gap in the curtains. Watched her gracefully mount her horse.

Her profile looked suitably regal in the silvery moonlight, especially up there on her horse. He felt like a peasant watching a queen, and it didn't even bother him. She looked like she *should* be a queen, and so far she'd been nothing but helpful. Kind.

The terrible part was he couldn't find a way to mistrust her.

Chapter Five

Mary had been raised to believe in integrity, no matter how hard it was to stand for the right thing. First, by her parents. Then by Jack.

Jack always made it look easy, and Mary had never struggled with it. Until now. Walker had given her enough information that she might be able to dig around to find out his last name and the details of his mother's murder.

But he didn't want her to. So she didn't.

Maybe it was common decency, or maybe it was the fact that she'd grown up in a small town where everyone felt entitled to every detail of her parents' disappearance whether she wanted them to or not.

Still, as she went about her day, she found her mind occupied with Walker's story, with what had happened in his apartment complex the morning before and wondering if he'd still be at the cabin when she went down there tonight.

And she wondered at the odd twist inside her that wanted him to be. She tried to convince herself it was the HSS mission, empathy for his situation, and it was. Partly.

But there was a part that had something to do with the way the silence between them had stretched out last night, and how her thoughts had wandered.

It wasn't that she'd never had thoughts about a man before. She had dated. Admittedly mostly in college, because it had been away from Sunrise and anyone who knew the story of her parents so intimately it infected every interaction. But she'd been more of a serial dater, never comfortable getting too deep into it. The two times she'd gotten close enough to sleep with someone, that had seemed to cure any desire to stay with them.

She liked her privacy. She liked her control.

She'd wondered what it would feel like to kiss Walker within twenty-four hours of meeting him, after people had shot at them, and she didn't know what to do with that. It wasn't...*her*.

"Hey."

Mary jumped nearly a foot, and then cursed herself for being so lost in thought. Especially since it was Anna scaring the tar out of her. Because Anna knew about Walker and would no doubt wonder if that's where Mary's thoughts had been.

Mary fixed a smile on her face and turned to Anna. "You scared me."

"Sexy daydreams do tend to distract a person."

Mary scowled. "Hardly." She wasn't going to bite. She was going to change the subject. "I haven't seen much of Hawk lately. Is he feeling all right?"

It was Anna's turn to scowl. "He's busy sneaking out doing things he shouldn't. You'd think a man who'd been shot within an inch of his life would learn to sit still."

"I would not think that of a man who married *you*."

Anna stuck out her tongue at Mary, but then her expression grew serious and Mary turned her attention back to the food she was preparing. Because Anna serious was not anything she wanted to deal with on a good day.

Not that it was a bad day. She was just unsettled.

"Are you sure about this whole Walker thing? Because

you don't usually get involved in…well, anything. And your mind never wanders. Maybe I should deal with Walker."

Mary didn't know why something dark and bitter settled within her, or why she allowed the snotty response. "Because I'm so incapable?"

"That is *not* what I said." Anna put her hand over Mary's busy ones until Mary looked up at her sister's serious hazel eyes. "You're probably the most capable out of all of us, but you don't like this stuff. You don't like getting involved. You like—or at least have spent most of your life convincing us that you like—being in the background."

"I prefer the background, yes. And I'm not changing that. This isn't a job. This is providing shelter for someone—which, I might add, *is* what I usually do."

Anna sighed heavily. "I see you're going to be stubborn, so there's no point arguing."

"Wow, pregnancy *has* matured you, Anna."

She snorted out a laugh, then fell into step helping Mary prepare dinner. It wasn't Anna's turn, but Mary wasn't going to refuse the help. Especially when Anna was doing it quietly and competently instead of her usual whirlwind of chatter and purposefully doing things in ways Mary did not do them.

"I'm only going to say one more thing about it," Anna said after a while of working in silence.

Mary fixed her sister with a disbelieving look until Anna grinned.

"Okay, one more thing *today*. If it gets too much, if you feel like you're in over your head, I can take over. Don't try to tackle this yourself just because I'm pregnant." She patted her little bump. "Little Hawklet has still got a while to bake yet."

"If you keep calling her that, we're going to end up using it, I hope you know that."

Anna laughed, but she sobered quickly, pinning Mary with an intense, serious gaze that immediately put Mary on edge.

"I hope you know you're the only reason having a girl doesn't freak me out," Anna said, with all the somber seriousness she almost never used. "That you're here, and I know you'll help. I'd be lost without you, Mary."

Mary kept very still, tried very hard not to be swallowed up by the emotions that brought out in her. But she had to be strong. The calm one. In control. Always. "Are we saying goodbye?"

"No, pregnancy makes me sappy and truthful," Anna replied with a shrug. "So, I wanted you to know." Then she pulled Mary into a tight hug.

Mary stood there and took it. She was too shocked to reciprocate. Anna was not demonstrative as a rule. Okay, none of them were.

Anna pulled back, and then laughed. Mary couldn't for the life of her figure out why. But Anna laughed all the way out of the kitchen.

WALKER PACED THE small if comfortable cabin, phone to his ear, trying to figure out what the hell he was going to do.

"I lost the tail," Carlyle said, with enough confidence the worry curdled in Walker's gut. She could be too confident. Too sure. It would get her into trouble one of these days out there on her own.

He never should have let her go. He'd known it had been a mistake, but last year she'd begged him. Poked at him and argued with him about the fact that she was an *adult* and blah, blah, blah.

He'd finally caved, and now he regretted it. "Can you get somewhere new without a tail?"

"What do you take me for?"

He didn't respond to that. He had to get her somewhere safe. Somewhere he could keep his damn eye on her. He looked around the cabin. It would be perfect.

But he'd have to clear it with Mary—which rankled. Then he'd have to make sure Carlyle got here without a tail. Then Mary and Carlyle would likely have some kind of interaction and for some reason he balked at that idea.

"Why did you hire these people anyway?" he muttered, before fully thinking the question through.

"Who? The HSS? Oh, I came across their website. They had all this experience, but it wasn't like one of those sketchy private investigator things. It was like…because they'd gone through it, they wanted to help people. And they were a family. It was like the rich, happy version of us. And you were…"

She trailed off. He didn't need her to rehash what he'd been. What he still was. On the trail of a killer. And he'd been getting close.

"It's been ten years, Walker," Carlyle said softly. "You're out there dodging bullets, and one of these days one is going to land. You're not getting any younger. I mean, you'll be forty before you know it."

He scowled into the phone. She really was irritating. "I think the nursing home is a ways off yet, Car."

"My point is, maybe you need help. We've been close for years. Maybe to get over that final hump, you need a little outside input."

He rested his forehead against the rough-hewn board of the cabin's interior wall. They didn't *need* help, but he could hear the note in Carlyle's voice she was usually too busy poking at him to let come through. She was tired. She was lonely. She hadn't had a normal life since she'd been twelve—no, scratch that. Moving around like fugitives as she'd done her entire childhood wasn't normal. She'd never known normal. And that wasn't all his fault.

But some of it was.

"Walker?"

"If I agree to get help, I want you here."

"In Nowhere, Wyoming? With you breathing down my neck?"

"Yeah. You and Zeke. If we're getting help, we need to stick together while we get it. We can't risk it otherwise."

There was a long pause, but he didn't rush her. Just because she wanted a normal life didn't mean she wanted to be with him again. Because, apparently, he was overbearing and unreasonable.

"Okay. If you promise to use the help, I'll convince Zeke. We'll have to make a pretty round-about trip out there to avoid any detection, but we'll get there in a few days."

They discussed details. He wouldn't have her come out to the Hudson Ranch right away. Once she and Zeke arrived in Bent County, he'd meet them somewhere remote. Bring them back, knowing for sure they didn't have a tail.

Mary seemed pretty sure the Hudsons could weather some danger, but Walker didn't feel right about being the one to bring them into the middle of his deal. None of this felt right.

"Don't have second thoughts, Walker," Carlyle said firmly in his ear. "We've done this your way all these years. It's time for a new way."

He didn't disagree exactly. He'd just prefer a new way that was all him and no one else. But he supposed that was the old way, all in all. "I'm going to have second thoughts the whole damn time, Car, but that doesn't mean I'm going to change my mind."

"Good, then I'm taking that as a promise. I'll talk to Zeke. We'll get in contact once we're close."

"All right. Be careful."

"I always am," she said cheerfully, which was a bold-faced lie, but what was he supposed to do about it?

"Yeah." He stood there, his forehead still pressed to the wall. He didn't want this, but it had been almost a year since he'd seen his siblings. So despite the part of him that dreaded what was coming, there was a small part of him just...glad. "It'll be good to see you, squirt."

"Yeah, but I don't want to hear anything about the new tattoo."

He groaned and she laughed as she hung up on him. He shoved the phone into his pocket. He only had a little battery power left. He wasn't about to ask Mary for any help in that department, but he wasn't quite sure what he was going to do about it yet.

He hated not being sure of his next steps, but his siblings joining him here... It was a lot to take in. A lot to accept.

And if he was being fully honest with himself, this was nice. Just him. No distractions, no worry. He'd actually slept last night, hard and long, and he couldn't remember the last time he'd done that.

He blew out a breath. He knew he couldn't get used to it. Mary might not want two more people hiding out here—though if they were using her family's company maybe that changed things.

Walker finally turned away from the wall. He felt nauseous at the thought of bringing in a company. Mary's family. People poking into his business, the case he'd been building for ten years.

Building and failing to find the one answer he still needed.

A sharp knock sounded at the door, and Walker thought about ignoring it. Would she bust in anyway? Or would she go the hell away?

But in the end, he answered it, because he'd told Carlyle he was going to accept help. And he wouldn't go back on his word. He'd promised that to Carlyle a long time ago. He'd broken a lot of promises to her since then, but never that one.

Mary swept in easily, carrying all sorts of things. "I brought some portable batteries if you need them. If you think you might stay for more than a few more days, I can get the electricity turned back on. I handle those kinds of admin processes, and if Jack asks I can always say it was a clerical error."

He stared at her as she set down a new cooler, a bag of batteries and whatever else. Every movement was careful, economical. When she was done and looked up at him, she clasped her hands in front of her, all neat and prim.

And far too beautiful for *his* own good.

He didn't want her family, up in that big house, poking through everything. Asking him questions it would only irritate him to answer. But he didn't mind *her*.

At all.

"Why'd you track me down to give me the money?" he asked, needing to understand how he'd wound up here. Maybe needing to understand some piece of *her*. "You could have kept it. I know it doesn't matter in the grand scheme of your empire here, but you had every right to keep it when you couldn't find us right away."

She didn't answer at first, though she didn't seem startled by the abrupt question. She stared at him very solemnly, as if deciding what to say. There was something about that stillness, that patience and quiet she had, that he would have assumed would make him uncomfortable or suspicious, but instead felt like peace.

"I have this memory…one of my first, I think, because Anna was a baby so I couldn't have been more than three," she said, and she spoke softly and calmly, with her mouth just barely curved upward. "We were at the county fair, I think. Some kind of thing like that, and my mother found a wallet on the ground. It had some money in it, I think, but no identification. My parents joked about it being their lucky day, but then we spent—well, what felt like to me as a little girl—half the day trying to track down the owner. And I don't know how many people told my dad to just keep it. But every time he'd just say to whoever it was, in this patient, calm drawl of his, 'It isn't the right thing to do.'"

He could hear the longing in her voice, how much she missed the man. What he'd meant to her. Walker didn't understand it. He'd hated his father, loved his mother—but God knew, she was complex, and even knowing he'd loved her didn't make him have a lot of fond memories of the way they'd lived.

"So every time I saw that money sitting in the account," Mary continued, "I'd just hear my father's voice. And my siblings all told me the same thing you did. Anytime I brought up wanting to track you down, everyone would point out if the money was needed or wanted, it'd be easy to return it. But I just kept hearing my father's voice."

"You miss him."

"Yes. I'm sure I always will. Don't you miss your mother?"

"I don't know. Seems these days I curse her half as much as I miss her."

"I think it's all missing."

"Maybe." He was uncomfortable with all this sincerity, so he might as well move the conversation along. "Listen, I talked to my sister about why she tried to hire you guys in the first place. She gave me the whole spiel about your family." He didn't mention the whole *like us, but rich* thing. "We've been stuck at this same place, close to finding out who killed our mother, but not getting there. Just making ourselves more of a target." Damn, that irked. "She wants to try you guys, and I told her... Well, I agreed anyway."

"Walker. That's wonderful. We can't promise results, but with our resources, we just have so much to offer. And a new set of eyes, an unbiased set of eyes, never hurts. It's Grant's turn to take on the next case, so—"

"No, not your siblings. You."

Her happy, earnest expression changed into one he couldn't read. But when she spoke it was calm and to the point. "I don't take on investigations. I don't... It's not my area of expertise." She shook her head, a little too emphatically to his way of thinking. "Grant would be better. He's a former marine and—"

But he didn't want her siblings, didn't trust them. "The only way I'm bringing in your family is if it's you. I don't want to talk to them. I don't trust them, but I trust you, Mary. God knows why."

Chapter Six

Mary couldn't remember the last time she'd been caught so off guard. It felt a little bit like being shot. Surprise and shock and then a little slice of pain.

"I don't investigate, Walker. I file things. I handle the accounts, the phone calls, the accommodations." She'd tried, once upon a time, but the failure of it all ate her up.

And that was the thing about cold cases. No matter how good HSS was, they couldn't always find answers. They hadn't even found answers when it came to their own parents.

She didn't have the heart for it, and if she couldn't find answers for Walker... It shouldn't, but it felt more personal. And she couldn't do it. "I do not investigate."

"So, now you do," he returned, as if he got to decide. As if he could flip a switch.

She wanted to be angry, she really did, but he said he trusted her. So instead of being angry she just felt a bit awed. And a bit trapped.

"If I..." She was not really thinking about agreeing to this, was she? "If I was the lead investigator for HSS, my siblings would still need to know about it. We work as a team, with a lead investigator who deals with the client and the actual investigating, but Palmer and Anna help with any computer research, and we bounce ideas off each other, and Grant and Jack handle law enforcement angles and—"

"That's fine." He shrugged. "Long as I only have to deal with you. And you all understand how dangerous it is."

Yes, I recall being shot at in your apartment just yesterday, she wanted to say. But she didn't allow herself snippy commentary if she could help it. "I'm not a big fan of danger," she said instead.

"We were shot at and you didn't even scream. You climbed out my window like a pro. You hopped in a car with a stranger. You've got that gunshot wound. Seems to me, you and danger are intimately acquainted."

There was something about the way he said *intimately* that made her want to blush, but she didn't. "I didn't say I was unaccustomed to danger. I said I wasn't a fan." She sounded overly prim even to herself.

"You don't have to take the job, Mary."

"And you don't have to make me be the lead investigator, Walker," she snapped in return, then winced a little as she hated when she got snappish.

"I've spent ten years doing this, Mary. Ten years. When the cops stopped, I couldn't. Even when I was trying to get Carlyle through high school, working in the damn school cafeteria to make ends meet and trying not worry about Zeke off in the army, I kept looking. I've been chasing leads for so long, I wouldn't know how to stop if I could. So, if I'm giving up ten years of full control and doing it my way and protecting my siblings, then it's damn well going to be the way I see fit."

His anger didn't poke at her own. Maybe because she understood. So fully. "I know what it's like, Walker. You don't have to prove how hard it is to me."

He blew out a frustrated breath. And she could see how

hard he was holding on because…because he was afraid of letting go. He was afraid. Period.

"All right. Then it's settled," he said, looking at her belligerently as if daring her to refuse.

She didn't want it to be settled, but she knew he needed help. She didn't want to be the one to give it to him, not like this, but… If it was the only way, she *had* to do it. And maybe she'd convince him. Maybe he'd come around to trust her family too. And all the while he'd be here and safe.

She ignored the odd impulse to cross the room and wrap her arms around him in a comforting hug. It wouldn't go over well, clearly. But more, she wasn't sure it was all innocent impulse on her part. "And you'll stay here?"

"As long as I think it's safe to—for your family and mine. My brother and sister are going to meet me here in a few days. Now, I don't want you thinking you have to feed us or—"

"Oh, you won't all fit in here. And with no electricity? If you come stay at the big house, we—"

"No big house. No family. This cabin and you. That's it. And we take care of ourselves. No more dinner packages. You don't need to turn on the electricity. We're resilient."

She frowned at him. "That's stubborn for the sake of being stubborn."

"Well, you and my siblings will get along just fine because I'm sure they'll think so too."

She wanted to laugh at that. How much his family sounded like hers. How she understood that no matter how similar they were, there was a difference. She'd had a support system. Not just because she was younger and she'd had older siblings to see her through. But the fact that she—and her siblings—had inherited this ranch. That her parents had the knowledge and economic standing to have it all in a trust so it passed to them with minimal issue. That no matter the hardship they'd gone through, no matter how her parents' disappearance still haunted them all, they hadn't spent their childhoods or adolescences struggling to make ends meet.

There had been an element of luck to her tragic circumstances, and it didn't seem like Walker and his siblings had run into much luck at all.

He was practically prowling the cabin now. "I mean it. No electricity, no more food. I'll handle it. I take care of my own."

She understood the impulse—to an extent. "Well, that's very nice and all, but I also take care. And I plan on bringing you meals because that's what *I* do. I'm going to have the electricity turned on because it's stupid not to. *I* am going to handle all of this how *I* see fit since you're insisting *I* be the lead investigator."

He glowered at her. "Then we're going to have a problem."

She didn't wilt at his glower. Honestly, did he think it was intimidating? No matter how dark his eyes were, or how impressive the arms crossed over his chest were, she did not feel intimidated. Other things, but not that. She lifted her chin. "Then I guess we are."

His expression turned speculative. "Anything ever rile you up?" he demanded.

"You're hardly the first man to ever ask me that, and I doubt you'll be the last. This is called maturity, Walker. And I have it in spades."

He looked at her, with the kind of belligerence she knew so well. Hurt pride and frustration. She'd seen it on all of her siblings' faces more often than she cared to count.

And she didn't have it in her to be a brick wall to that. Not when she'd spent her entire life being the soft place to land for the people in her life—because nowhere else was soft. Not really.

So she did cross to him then, no matter how many re-criminations her mind gave her. *He's a stranger. He's dangerous. He's not your responsibility. At best he's a client who's emotionally manipulated you into taking on tasks you don't want.*

But he was also a man in need of help. In need of that soft place to land, and Mary was never any good at not being that.

"We aren't enemies, Walker," she said, speaking in the same tone she might have used on any of her brothers as she reached out and put a comforting hand on his crossed arms. Except this close to him, looking up at his stormy dark eyes, feeling the powerful, tensed muscle of his arm, she didn't feel particularly sisterly. But that was neither here nor there. She focused on the task at hand. "We don't have to fight. We don't have to rile each other up. We're on the same team."

"In my life, all those things *do* mean being on the same team."

Which made her laugh because she understood that well enough. And for some reason, she didn't think to pull her hand away. She just stood there, a shade too close. And he stood there, looking at her a shade too intensely.

For way longer than could possibly be socially appropriate.

She stepped back, heart beating double time and sure she was being a complete and utter idiot. She retreated to the careful, icy demeanor she'd spent almost a lifetime perfecting.

"I'll come back tomorrow. Let's say ten? I'll get the paperwork started on moving the case forward with HSS."

He didn't say anything, didn't move for the longest time, and she fought off the urge to turn and run.

She wasn't a coward.

But eventually, all he said was "sure." And she turned and walked back to her horse. And if she thought she caught a glimpse of him watching her through the gap in the curtains, she swiped that thought away as foolish.

Whatever strange reactions she had to him were one-sided, obviously. And now he was a client. So there'd be no more thinking about his strong arms and his piercing eyes.

Period.

WALKER HAD WANTED to kiss her last night. A strange, unbidden urge that held him in a grip so strong he'd nearly forgotten himself. Who he was, why he was here. All he could see was her, all he could want was her—this woman he barely knew.

He wasn't a man who spent a lot of time deliberating when he could act—when action, even mistaken action, often moved the needle forward. And he trusted his gut.

His gut seemed to know her—whether his brain agreed or not.

Then she'd stepped back and plastered on that cool, queen-of-the-manor smile.

Which was for the best. Getting mixed up in Mary Hudson would no doubt be a fatal mistake.

Why was he getting help from her again? It didn't seem to matter if she was talking in that cool, calm voice of hers with her hands clasped, or looking up at him with soft brown eyes, or firming her mouth in a kind of frustrated disapproval.

She did something to him, and he did *not* have time for that. Didn't like the way it distracted him from the complicated tasks at hand.

Bringing people in didn't give him less work, it gave him more. He had to decide what to share, and how. Had to think about the ways he gave Mary information, as she'd no doubt share it with her family.

She'd called it a *case*. It wasn't a *case*. It was murder. Life and death. His.

And now maybe even her?

He scowled at that damn voice in his head. She'd been the one to push her way in. If meeting him under the rain of bullets didn't clue her in that this was a dangerous thing to get involved in, he didn't know what would.

He glanced at his watch. He'd been useless all morning because she'd said she'd be here at ten, and what the hell was he supposed to do? Right now his next steps involved waiting on his siblings, and waiting on Mary Hudson and her HSS.

He hated waiting. But he knew well that what he hated didn't matter in the grand scheme of the universe. Because the universe did whatever it damn well pleased.

Half resigned, half infuriated, Walker marched over to the window and glanced out the curtain gap. In the distance, he could see a graceful figure on top of a horse crest the hill.

Why his body tightened, why his heartbeat sped up a little bit was so utterly beyond him he didn't know what to do about it. Nothing about Mary Hudson should get under his skin.

But everything seemed to. He turned away from the window, called it self-preservation over cowardice and waited for her knock at the door.

When it came, he just hollered a "come in" because if he answered the door he was half-afraid he'd be tempted to grab her like some kind of Neanderthal.

She slid in, all quiet, efficient movements. "Good morning," she greeted cheerfully. She had a little satchel tucked under her arm. As usual, she looked neat as a pin. Yesterday she'd been dressed a bit more casually than the day before—jeans and a blouse rather than the flowy skirt. Today was more back to the office. A boxy skirt, sensible shoes, a fussy blouse and pulled-back hair.

He'd never considered prim and proper his type before, but something about Mary made it seem downright mouth-watering.

And so not the point of this little exercise, he reminded himself. She was here to help, when he'd given up on help years ago when the detectives on his mother's case had, more or less, told him to stop wasting their time.

Mary moved into the room, put her satchel on the table and began to unpack its contents. File folders and note-books and pens and pencils, and just when he'd been about to make a quip about it being the twenty-first century, she pulled out a small tablet.

Walker stood half a room away, leaning against the wall, arms crossed over his chest as a reminder of where his hands should stay. "That's a lot," he said, because he was afraid he'd find himself commenting on how fresh she looked if he didn't say something disdainful.

"An investigation's first and best tool is organization," she returned in that equally bright manner.

He wanted to laugh. He didn't agree for a lot of reasons. The top being neither he nor his siblings had the first clue how to organize anything.

He could fight. He could shoot a gun. He could jump out of buildings and protect his siblings. But he'd never been so happy as the day Carlyle had graduated high school and he hadn't had to worry about permission slips, the right color folders or calls from teachers about missing assignments.

"This feels like school," he said.

She looked up at him, and she did remind him of a teacher. One of the ones who would have given him a kind lecture about understanding the difficult position he was in but needing Carlyle to put forth more effort.

Like he'd ever been able to get that wildling to do anything.

"Well, you're in luck. I excelled at school."

"I just bet you did," he muttered.

"You know, we'd accomplish more if you'd meet me up at the main house," she said, sitting now that all her little pads and notebooks and pens were arranged.

"Too risky yet."

"What exactly are you waiting on?"

"My siblings to get here and to know they weren't followed." He didn't have to divulge the next part. Even if she was agreeing to help, it didn't mean she was a full-on partner in his family's mess. But no matter how he told himself to be circumspect, the truth came out anyway. "And my brother to have a lead on who tried to take me out the other day."

"Do you really believe they were trying to take you out?" she asked, pen poised at the paper like she was about to take notes.

"Huh?"

"Well, it's just…" Mary pursed her lips, looking thoughtful. "I've gone over the events of the day from my perspective many times. It seems to me, someone who really wanted you dead wouldn't go shooting up your apartment in the morning. They'd have someone break in late at night when you might be asleep. They'd have some kind of sniper situation. There would have been men at all the exits of your apartment."

He'd, of course, considered these things, then dismissed them as sloppy work. "I think you messed with their plans."

"Maybe. But you have a murder that you've been trying to solve for ten years. And I'm not saying you aren't good at dodging danger, but…" She tapped her fingers on the table. "I don't know. Something doesn't add up."

Walker didn't have anything to say to that because he didn't disagree. Something *didn't* add up. It never had.

"But that's usually how cold cases go. Though if someone is after you, it's not so cold, is it?"

He didn't bother to answer that, since he didn't get the impression she was talking to him. She was making notes on little preprinted pages in a binder.

"Your father would have been the first person the police looked at back then?"

"Yeah."

She looked up from her little notebook. There was enough pity there to have him bristling.

"No need to be careful about it. Did it bother me that they'd look at the guy who knocked my mom, my brother and me around for years? No, Mary. Weirdly I was right on board."

She stared at him for a full beat, all that coolness wrapped around her like a cloak. It made him feel like a dick when he didn't particularly want to analyze his own behavior at the moment.

"Unfortunately, it was a dead end. In a lot of ways. Dad had ties to a gang called Sons of the Badlands. The cops and I followed that thread for a while, but it never really panned out. If anything, I think it took us farther from whatever the truth is. The gang doesn't even exist anymore. Wiped out a few years back, so whoever is after me can't be them."

"Unless they were just affiliated but maybe not as involved. But you'd have thought of that, poked into that."

"Yeah."

"Do you have any files? Notes? Lists?"

It was probably perverse of him that he looked forward to showing her. "Sure." He went to the room he'd been sleeping in and grabbed the duffel he shoved things into when he found things he meant to keep. In the old days, he'd handed that sort of thing off to Zeke, but he hadn't seen his brother in so long he'd accumulated quite a bit.

He returned to the table, and then upended the entire contents there in front of her. All crumpled papers and sloppy writing and a slew of things that likely only made sense to him.

He would have felt badly about it—if he'd had some other way of doing it, if he wasn't feeling rubbed raw from sharing all this in the first place, and if she didn't just survey the pile of papers without even a blink.

When she spoke, it was patient scolding. "Walker," she said, as if he'd just presented her with a dead mouse like a house cat.

"Yeah?"

"I don't suppose you have something more…organized? A computer file or…"

He tapped his temple. "The only computer file I need."

"Your siblings then? They have something more tangible?"

Zeke did, but Walker shrugged. "Maybe."

She nodded. "Well, that's something. I guess we should sort through this and make sense of it." She didn't seem irritated by that. She seemed almost…excited. "And once we're done, you'll have a much more organized situation. I'll have to remember a binder tomorrow. Unless you prefer to keep everything here with you?"

"I can't say as I care one way or another. Like I said, the important information is up here." He tapped his temple once more.

"Yes, of course. But you have help now. The more eyes that can look at the information displayed in an organized, sensible manner, the better chance we have of finding something new to go on."

He supposed that made sense, even if it gave him an itch between his shoulder blades. If he hadn't promised Carlyle, he probably would have put it all back into the bag and told her to go.

As it was, all he could do was shove his hands into his pockets and watch Mary. "I guess I should help or something?"

"Not yet. I'm working up a system. I'll have some questions soon." She smiled up at him over a stack of papers. "I love to put order to things." And she wasn't lying. He could tell by how genuine that smile was.

The thought of trying to make order out of that mess made him want to run in the opposite direction. "You're a strange lady."

"Yes, so I've been told. Usually by people who will benefit from my excellent organization skills. Is your last name really Daniels?" she asked casually, already sorting through things, smoothing out crumpled papers and stacking them in a neat pile.

"Yeah," he muttered.

She didn't react to that information, just kept organizing and even started humming to herself.

She was clearly in her element and while it didn't make a lick of sense to him, he found himself watching her, mesmerized. Not by the efficient movements or even the humming.

It was the smile on her face. It was all that cool control he couldn't seem to get under—and both the admiration and frustration he felt in the face of it. And then there was something underneath all that—something he would have called a gut feeling if it had been bad.

But it wasn't. It was a very simple want.

He wanted it to be simple anyway. Because it wasn't that he *never* took any time for himself. When there were lulls in the case, he went out in the world and blew off some steam and had a good time. He wasn't a joyless robot—as Carlyle had once accused Zeke of being.

The problem was this was no lull, and Mary was no bar pickup. He'd always compartmentalized his life quite well. But Mary felt like soap to all that oil and water. She was mixing everything up.

"You don't have to watch me," she muttered after a while, though she'd never once looked up from her work. She was standing now, almost done turning the mound of papers into neat little piles.

"If it helps, I'm not watching you, per se."

"Oh, really, then what are you doing?"

He knew he should stop. Knew he shouldn't let that prim, cool question allow the lines to blur.

But if knowing something stopped people from doing things, there'd be a lot fewer problems in the world.

"Thinking about kissing you, actually."

He watched her reaction carefully. Wondering if she'd go all cool, or if she'd finally be irritated enough with him to fully snap.

She did still, but her cheeks turned a dark shade of pink. She cleared her throat and rearranged some papers he was pretty sure had already been arranged.

And said nothing. Which made him think that maybe, just maybe, his little ice queen had been thinking a bit about kissing him.

Since that amused him, he didn't let it go. "Just going to let that sit there, huh?"

"What else am I supposed to do?" she said, and there was a snap to her tone as she glared at him. "Kiss a man I barely know over all this paperwork about his mother's murder?"

Well, she could land a blow when she wanted to, couldn't she? He figured it was supposed to knock him back a step, but he'd grown up too rough not to admire a well-placed barb when it was deserved.

"This is like college all over again," she said, and her movements were agitated now, even as she reconcentrated on her little piles.

He could not for the life of him make sense of her comment. "You're going to need to explain that to me."

She blew out a frustrated breath, her hair fluttering with the move. This was definitely getting to her, and it was fascinating. The slow unravel.

"It's just… In Sunrise, everyone knows who I am. What I am. I went off to college and all the rules were different. People didn't know or care that I was Jack Hudson's little sister. Or Anna's boring big sister."

"You don't strike me as boring, Mary. Considering you didn't scream or fall apart when men were shooting at us for reasons you didn't even know."

She opened her mouth as if to make a counterpoint, but then she simply shut it. She looked at him with an expression he couldn't read. Something in his chest twisted and he realized he *wanted* to read it. Wanted to understand what put that odd cast to her eyes.

He knew he should keep his distance. He knew he should extricate himself from this conversation. But he moved toward her. He didn't stop it.

"You just don't understand," she insisted. So seriously, so intensely. Like it was an important truth she had to hang her hat on. "At least here in this little microcosm, I can't just be a random woman you think about…kissing." Her blush deepened, and she practically squeaked out the word. "I'm Jack the sheriff's sister, pretty intimidating. Or Anna's sister, not as pretty, not as interesting. I'm Dean and Laura

Hudson's daughter—the *missing* and likely long dead Dean and Laura Hudson, that is. I can't just be—"

"You?" he supplied.

She sucked in a sharp breath, then let it out. Some of her mask was coming back. "I guess. But the thing is, I left. I went to college. And I didn't like it. I didn't like being away from home or my family or even those things I always looked at as negatives. I don't like the order of things upended. I *like* the way people see me here."

"Even if it isn't you?"

"That's the thing. It *is* me. It is all the things that make up me. And I like it better when people know, when they understand, when they…"

He heard a lot of words, a lot of insecurities in all this. He wasn't sure what it had to do with kissing her except that little bit about *the order of things*. She was careful. She was controlled.

And when other people were involved, as he knew all too well, your control got blown to hell. And sometimes it was easier to keep that distance than lose what little control you had on life.

"You like it better that way because that's when people stay at a safe distance?" He supposed, since he understood, he should stay at that safe distance.

But he didn't. He stepped closer. They might still be closer to strangers than anything else, but if he knew anything about Mary Hudson, it was that she didn't back down.

And she didn't. Even when her expression was a little lost as she looked up at him with a kind of sadness in her eyes. "I don't know how to navigate these things. The right course of action or how you're supposed to…"

"I've never heard anyone, not once in my life, use the word *navigate* or the phrase *course of action* to discuss kissing or attraction."

"Because I don't know how to *do* this sort of thing. You look at me like that, say things like that. What the hell am I supposed to do?"

"How about this?" And then he went ahead and blew it all to hell and put his mouth to hers.

Chapter Seven

Mary had been kissed before. She tried to remind herself of this as Walker's mouth touched hers. As every last thought seemed to drain out of her mind. As his arms slid around her and drew her close and her whole body just relaxed into the great hard wall of him.

She forgot she shouldn't be kissing him. Forgot he was essentially a stranger. Because there was something just right about this moment. Like she'd been waiting for it, long before she'd ever laid eyes on Walker Daniels.

She had kissed men, rebuffed men. She knew how to handle people. She was an expert at getting exactly what she wanted out of a situation.

Which was probably the problem. Kissing him was like exploring some new world and she didn't have the first clue what she wanted out of it.

Except more.

His hands tangled in her hair and she slid her palms against the rough scrape of his unshaven jaw. Something hot, dangerous and wholly out of her control slithered through her. She dimly thought she should hate it, but it was too big, too right. Like she'd finally found something she'd been searching for all along.

He pulled gently away, and her heart was hammering and her pulse scrambling and every last cell of her body was alive with some kind of impossible buzzing.

Walker was still essentially a stranger, and he'd kissed her. She'd kissed him back. She wanted to keep kissing him. When his mouth was on hers, she didn't feel the need to keep her hands so tightly on the reins of control.

Which was dangerous. So she opened her eyes, tried to find some of her usual command of a situation. Instead, she froze as, over Walker's shoulder, her gaze met the gray-blue eyes of a woman she didn't recognize. Just standing there in the doorway.

They weren't alone.

She cleared her throat. "Walker."

If she was gratified by anything in this very strange day of her life, it was the fact that clearly the kiss had affected him almost as much as it had her. He didn't move, didn't seem to realize they were being watched. His gaze was on her, like she was a puzzle he wanted to solve.

Or undress.

"Yeah?"

"There's a woman staring at us."

He turned slowly, though he didn't let her go.

"So, this is why you finally agreed to help." The woman eyed Mary up and down, but it wasn't malicious exactly. "Nice work, lady."

"Oh, well." Mary couldn't think of anything to say. Her brain was completely and utterly blank.

Walker's hands dropped then as he fully turned toward the woman. "What are you doing here? I told you to—"

A man entered behind the woman—and there was no doubt this was Walker's brother, which likely made the woman his sister. Walker and the man looked so much alike, carbon copies of each other. Dark features and big frames and a sort of grim wildness about them, wrapped up in a very careful, assessing package.

"Yeah, plans had to change," he said to Walker. His gaze

flicked over Mary so fast she wasn't even sure it happened. "Things are getting a little hot. What did you stumble onto?"

"Stumble?" Walker scoffed as he walked over to them. "I don't stumble."

She knew sibling devotion. She had it. She was a part of it every day, and maybe that's what made witnessing this scene all the more poignant.

They wrapped their arms around each other. A trio. A unit. Clearly they hadn't seen each other in a while, and no matter the reasons they were seeing each other now, they were glad.

"Where's this new tattoo?" Walker asked the woman roughly.

"Don't worry about it." She nodded over at Mary. "You going to introduce us to your lip-lock partner, or what?"

Mary felt very out of place, and if they weren't huddled in the doorway, she likely would have escaped. But she was going to have to meet them eventually, discuss the case with them eventually.

Tell Jack about them sooner rather than later.

"Mary, this is my brother, Zeke. My sister, Carlyle. Guys, this is Mary Hudson. She's the HSS investigator Carlyle conned me into hiring."

"Not into kissing though."

"Knock it off, Car," Walker said, but it was all affection. There was a softness to him Mary hadn't witnessed—even during that kiss. Which hadn't been soft at all.

She really couldn't think about it. Not with all three Daniels siblings staring at her. So she clasped her hands, fixed a smile to her face. "Well, I'll extend the offer to the both of you that Walker refused. You're welcome to come stay at the main house. You don't need to rough it out here. But, if that's what you prefer, we'll be happy to accommodate."

"I'll stay at the main house," Carlyle said.

"No, you won't," Walker returned, a kind of authoritative growl Mary recognized as an older-brother thing.

Carlyle was clearly not impressed or swayed by it. "I'm not shoving in with you two grunting males. I escaped that, remember? Not going back unless we absolutely have to. And Mary here says we don't."

Walker glared at his sister, but she seemed impervious. She reminded Mary of Anna, though maybe a little more feral, and that made Mary smile.

"Well, then I'll take you up, Carlyle," Mary said, smiling blandly at Walker, even as he narrowed his eyes at her. "Perhaps you'd all consider coming to the big house for dinner so we can discuss the case." She began to arrange her piles together, slide them into the satchel. She'd look through them with Grant later, formulate a list of questions and threads to pull. Organize them into a binder.

She had a plan, and kissing Walker hadn't changed it.

"Dinner? Sounds fun," Carlyle said, grinning at her brothers—who clearly did not look like they thought it would be fun. But they didn't argue with her, so Mary tucked her satchel under her arm and moved over to the trio.

"Carlyle, how do you feel about horses?"

"Intrigued," she returned.

So Mary led her outside to Pippi, and gave Carlyle her first horseback ride. All the while deciding how she was going to explain the Daniels clan to her family.

And putting Walker's kiss as far out of her mind as possible.

WALKER WATCHED THEM GO. A lot of different emotions were twisting deep in his gut.

There was Carlyle, who he hadn't seen in a year, already swanning off to the Hudson residence and agreeing to dinner and more connection than he'd wanted to allow.

And Zeke, standing right next to him. As tall as him now. He'd lived his own life for years, having been seventeen when their mother was murdered. He'd done some work in the military, worked for some secret organization after that and was now fully dedicated, like Walker, to finding answers.

Walker worried about his brother, who he was quite certain never got distracted by pretty women or fun of any kind.

And speaking of women… There was Mary herself—a conundrum, one he couldn't even keep to himself because his siblings had seen evidence. He watched Mary and his sister disappear over the hill.

"I don't like it," he muttered.

"Why? Think Car's going to chew her up and spit her out?" Zeke asked, his thoughts on the matter carefully hidden behind a dry delivery.

"Mary can hold her own," Walker returned irritably. Carlyle was a pill, but she wasn't mean. Usually. Regardless, Mary was a handler. Even if Car proved to be a challenge, Mary would rise to the occasion. He had no doubt.

"Didn't look like it," Zeke said.

The comment shouldn't make him want to defend Mary, but he did. "Yeah, well, she's surprising like that."

"Something I should be concerned about?"

"What would be the concern?"

"That you're getting yourself wrapped up in a romance instead of a murder investigation."

Walker laughed. It was the word *romance*, which was so ludicrous he couldn't do anything but laugh. Still, his brother's harsh tone didn't amuse him. If anything, it worried him.

"I can kiss a woman and investigate all at the same time, and if you can't, you might want to reconsider your life choices."

Zeke scowled. "I know Car's the one who pushed for help, and I can see you're on board, but I've still got some reservations."

"You wouldn't be you if you didn't. I've still got reservations myself." And they'd been made more complicated by kissing Mary, but Zeke didn't need to know that. "Why did you come right away when I told you to wait? I wanted to make sure—"

"I know, I know. That we weren't followed. That's the problem. I almost didn't see my tail, but I picked him up over in Cody. I called in a friend from my North Star days. Got the tail off me over in Hardy by using him as a body double, but these guys were close and careful. So, Car and I had to act fast before they caught wind again. We've got to hunker down real low until we're sure what we want our next steps to be, and I think those steps should be together. Even if Carlyle hates the idea."

"Agreed there."

"But adding all these people isn't exactly laying low, is it?"

"They're trained investigators, Zeke. Been at this even longer than us and they are far more organized and connected." And why the hell was he defending them when he hadn't wanted to use them in the first place? But he'd promised Carlyle, and... Well, if it had something to do with Mary, so what? "They know how to lay low, and I've explained to Mary how dangerous it is. She stumbled into it quite by accident. She was there when they shot at me."

Zeke's eyebrows rose at that.

"And she held her own. She's not quite as delicate as she appears."

"I'm going to repeat myself. Is this something I should be concerned about?"

The whole warm, loving sensation of actually seeing his

siblings in person for the first time in a year was starting to wear off. Real quick.

"Do you not trust me, Zeke?" Walker said in his off-handed way. He didn't let any of the tension winding through him leak out in his voice.

Zeke grunted irritably. "I've seen a few too many people do dumb shit over soft feelings for someone."

Soft feelings. He wasn't sure that's how he'd character-ize what he felt for Mary. That kiss had been a little more complicated than soft, but there was enough truth there, and enough worry he *would* end up doing something stupid, he could hardly fault his brother for the concern.

So he changed the subject. "Carlyle pushed for this. She won't say it. Maybe she hasn't even admitted it to herself, but I can hear it. She's tired. She's lonely. She's almost twenty-three years old and hasn't had a second of normal. I'd like to live long enough to give her some normal."

Zeke only grunted in response.

"Maybe this HSS doesn't do anything for us. What's the harm? They get me killed? I've spent years keeping myself from that eventuality. I can keep doing it."

"You trying to convince me or yourself?"

Walker laughed, clapped his brother on the shoulder. "Both of us, obviously."

Zeke almost cracked a smile. But it quickly morphed back into a frown and he sighed. "We're going to have to go for dinner."

"Why the hell would we do that?" Walker replied, shocked his brother would even suggest it. He didn't want to be cozy-ing up to the Hudsons any more than he had to.

Or you want to keep your distance from Mary since you can't seem to keep your mouth to yourself.

Well, maybe some of both.

"We can't leave Carlyle alone with those people for too

long," Zeke said. "She's a feral raccoon at best. And those fancy digs up there? Not feral raccoon material."

Zeke wasn't exactly wrong, but as Walker himself also wasn't much better than a feral varmint, the comment stuck under his skin. "You're too hard on her."

"You indulge her."

An old argument, so old, so part of who they'd become that it felt good to have it. Familiar and right. And somehow, together, he figured they'd done okay. Carlyle wasn't perfect, but she was definitely her own woman.

For good or for ill.

Walker heaved out a sigh. "All right then. Let's go."

Chapter Eight

Mary settled Carlyle into one of the guest rooms. The woman didn't have much, but she seemed comfortable enough. Mary tried to get a read on the young woman, but it was difficult. Though she did remind Mary of Anna, there was something harder about Carlyle. And more… Well, the only word she could think of was *wild*. Just like Walker himself. Like nothing had quite tamed them into fitting in with the world.

Mary didn't know why that made her feel strangely protective of them. After all, Walker had been the protector when it came to that shooting in his apartment, and his siblings were obviously equal to the task of taking care of themselves.

But they just seemed in need of some tending.

"If your brothers decide to come for dinner—"

"Oh, they'll come," Carlyle replied, peering out the window, then back at Mary.

Mary was a little taken aback by Carlyle's certainty. Usually, she wouldn't press on a client. It was her job to smooth things over and make everyone comfortable. Not dig deeper. But… "How do you know?"

"Because the thought of me up here, by myself, doing what I do—which is often saying whatever I want to say, no matter how inappropriate—will shock and concern them both enough to do what they don't want to and come up here to play nanny and chaperone." She took a seat on the bed, gave it a little bounce. "They'll both sleep out in that cabin to be stubborn, and they won't be able to talk me into joining them, though they'll try. But I'm just as stubborn as they are."

"I told Walker he was stubborn for the sake of being stubborn."

"That's a Daniels specialty," Carlyle said. Proudly. But then she fixed Mary with a certain kind of considering stare that made Mary want to fidget.

She didn't, of course.

"So, should I ask you your intentions with my brother?"

Mary tried very hard not to react. She'd spent a lifetime with Anna so she knew what it was like to deal with people who wanted to shock you. Still, when it came to Walker, her usual impervious mask was hard to hold on to. "Intentions?"

"You're just not really his type." She cocked her head, studying Mary as if she could determine what Walker might see in her. "So I was just wondering what you were getting out of the whole thing."

Mary's chin lifted. She tried to soften her expression, but it was difficult. It shouldn't put her back up—because it was *meant* to—but she didn't really want to hear about Walker's *type*. "I'm sure growing up the way you have, you're all very protective of one another. I can appreciate that. My siblings have a similar relationship."

"That's not an answer."

"No, it isn't," Mary replied. Firmly.

Carlyle laughed. "I just might like you, Mary."

"Yes. Well." What was there to say to that? Or about her intentions? Nothing. But there was plenty to say about the tasks at hand.

"I understand that your brothers are reluctant. And I'm sure there's nothing I can say to either of them to make them feel like involving HSS is a good idea. They're doing it for you."

Carlyle got a strange look on her face at that.

"So, I just wanted to say that I hope *you* feel confident in working with us and understand that my family and I can't possibly promise results, but we do promise to work very hard toward finding answers."

Carlyle didn't move, didn't break eye contact. Just studied Mary, as if is she watched long enough, she'd catch her in a lie. "Do you remember your parents?" she asked after a long stretch of quiet.

Mary was taken off guard but knowing that Carlyle had been through something similar with her parents softened her more than alarmed her. "Yes. I was ten years old when they disappeared. Some days it feels like they're slipping away and I barely remember what their voices sounded like, and some days it's like that was yesterday. I can smell them, hear them, feel them. I didn't go through exactly what you went through, Carlyle, but I understand. And I'll do everything I can to get you the answers you all deserve."

Carlyle breathed out a sigh and looked around the room. "I'm not sure what anyone deserves." She shook her head. "I love my brothers. I'm acutely aware of how much they gave up for me, and how hard they tried to make sure I didn't know that. They're both a pain in my ass, but they're the best men I've ever met. And they've been doing this too long. Walker is getting too close. He's going to get himself killed, and I think…I think in the back of his head, he's okay with that, if it gets us answers."

Mary felt her heart stutter at that. "I would not be okay with that," she said, though God knew why. She'd known the man for no time at all. And yes, he'd kissed her, and yes, she understood his life—and vice versa—in ways it was difficult for others to, but…

But what?

"Yeah, I'm not okay with it either. That's why I first contacted you guys. I want them safe. I want Walker safe." She finally met Mary's gaze again. "And you complicate that."

Mary blinked, taken aback. "How?"

"Well, if he's kissing you, I imagine that means he'll be wanting to keep *you* safe. So, he'll do a bunch of dumb macho stuff to ensure that you are. And no offense, Mary, you don't seem like the type of woman who knows how to keep herself safe."

Mary tried not to be offended, but it didn't work. "You'd be surprised what type of woman I am, Carlyle. Now, I have some work to do and dinner to prepare. You're free to use whatever facilities you see fit. If you're hungry, we'll eat in the dining room at six."

And Mary, far more impolitely than she should have been, turned and left, without even asking if Carlyle had any questions.

MARY PUT ALL her discomfort, worry and anxiety into preparing dinner. The familiar preparations soothed her—and took her mind off what Walker expected her to do.

And telling Jack about…everything.

Until Jack came into the kitchen, as he often did about fifteen minutes before dinner. To catch up on the day.

Jack was almost eight years older than her, but somehow they'd become the de facto parents of the family. Even if she was younger, she was the oldest girl. So they, probably more than anyone else, conferred and worked in tandem.

"Why are there three extra plates set for dinner?" he asked casually.

Mary looked up from her cooking preparations. He was dressed in his sheriff's uniform—utility pants and a perfectly pressed polo shirt with the Sunrise SD logo on it. He looked the same as he always did, but the older he got, the more he looked like their father.

Which made her feel extra guilty. It reminded her of when she'd made all the plans to leave to go to college in secret—because she hadn't wanted to tell Jack she was leaving. Hadn't wanted to face his wanting her to stay.

He'd been wonderful and supportive, of course, but Mary supposed she was always waiting to disappoint him somehow.

Who knew why. It really didn't bear thinking about.

So she fixed a smile on her face. "We have some new HSS clients and I invited them to dinner. One of them is going to stay in the big house with us, and the other two are going to stay out in the foreman's cabin."

Jack frowned. "This is a lot of new information I haven't heard anything about."

"You've been at work. It's been an…evolving situation."

"What's the case?"

"A murder from ten years ago. The kids of the murdered woman have been looking into it on their own and have gotten close, but no clear breaks."

"Grant taking lead?"

Mary looked back at her roast, began to get out the serving plates. "Well…"

"It's his turn."

"Yes, it is, but there's a slight…hiccup there. It's been requested that I be the lead investigator on this case." She counted out forks.

"You don't investigate."

"Not as a rule, no," Mary agreed easily as she shooed him out of the way so she could open the oven and pull the roast out. "But this time I will be."

Jack was quiet, and the silence stretched out, but Mary focused on transferring the roast to the serving platter. On sprinkling some cheese on top of the twice-baked potatoes. On anything but Jack.

"Mary…"

"I can handle an investigation now and again. It's hardly something to get hung up on. They've done a lot of work themselves, so it's more helping to organize, maybe finding a pattern they haven't noticed. I'll be consulting you all. In fact, I've already got Anna compiling some things for me. Nothing to concern yourself over."

"You may be able to fool the rest of them, but I was there." She hated that his voice was soft, gentle. Hated that she knew exactly what he was referring to.

"I was eighteen," Mary returned. She'd insisted she be given a case back then, before she'd left for college. She'd insisted Jack let her in because she'd wanted to be a part of it. Wanted to help, see if maybe she could swallow the idea of staying in Sunrise. She'd wanted to do more than cook and clean and organize.

At the time.

But she hadn't been able to take it. No matter how she'd dug, how many questions she'd asked, how many hours she'd put in, she'd never been able to find answers on that case he'd given her.

Then Jack had swept in and found them in twenty-four hours. He'd never acted disappointed—but how could he have not been?

"Yes. I believe I even pointed out your age at the time," Jack returned. Still way too gently. "And you vowed to never, ever, no matter what, take on another case. That it wasn't for you. You were very adamant."

Mary turned to face her brother, because facing him down was the only way she got through to him. "Yes. And at the time, I felt all that. But I'm older now. I understand more. I went away to college and learned something about…

failing on my own without someone to sweep up my mistakes."

"Name one time you've failed since you came back home." He smiled a little, but Mary didn't find it funny. It made her chest seize. She wanted to turn away and cry.

But Hudsons had never had that luxury. She pointed at her arm, where she'd been shot last month. "Palmer and Anna knew not to run out there. I was the dumb one."

His smile died. "It isn't dumb to want to save your brother and niece."

"It was in the moment. I should have known better. I fail now and again, and I may very well fail this. But they wanted me or they weren't going to accept help and they need help."

"It isn't your job to save everyone."

Mary cocked her head and narrowed her eyes. "Because it's yours?"

Jack sighed. Heavily. "I'll go get washed up if that's all the news."

"It is."

He moved to leave but paused in the doorway, then looked back at her. "Why do they want *you* to do it?"

"Because I'm the one who tracked them down about the money. The Joe Beck money, if you recall. I guess that lends me an air of trustworthiness to them. It's a complicated case, and a dangerous one."

Jack nodded thoughtfully, and it gave Mary too much time to think. To worry. To want to smooth it all over.

"They're three siblings and they're coming to dinner. I just want you to be…"

Jack raised an eyebrow, waiting for her to finish the sentence. But Mary was struggling to find the right word.

"How about nice?" she said finally. She smiled brightly while he continued to stare blankly at her.

"I'm always nice," he finally said flatly.

She was sure he thought that about himself, but poor Jack was hopelessly un-self-aware. It came from too many years of putting others first. Yes, she knew a bit about that. "No. You're always polite. There's a difference."

He scowled at her, so she smiled cheerfully even though she didn't feel cheerful. Or happy. She felt strung tight. Anxious and twisted in a million knots most decidedly not under her control.

But no one would ever know that.

Chapter Nine

Walker stared at the big, cozy-looking house in front of him, hands shoved deep in his pockets. When he glanced over at Zeke, his brother was in the same stance.

"We could just let Carlyle horrify them all," Zeke said after a while.

Walker sighed. It was tempting. Certainly better than trying to run herd on the demon that was his baby sister. But as annoying as it might be, this wasn't so much about Carlyle's feral manners as it was about what Carlyle might say to Mary that could alter Mary's opinion of him.

Not that he had any clue what Mary's actual opinion of him was, or why he was letting that matter.

Before he could say anything or make a decision either way, he heard a dog bark, followed by another and then another. He turned to look and saw two people and three dogs walking toward the house. And toward him and Zeke.

It must be more of Mary's family, and Walker didn't know why that made him tense. He usually didn't worry about handling people—he'd spent a lifetime learning how to maneuver, charm and get what he wanted out of just about anyone.

But everything about the Hudson Ranch made him feel like someone else altogether.

The man approached and stopped in front of them. It

didn't take any great detective work to identify him as one of Mary's brothers—and not the cop. He was tall and broad, but scruffy. His gaze was assessing like a cop, but there was something else about him that didn't give off cop or military vibes.

The little girl behind him that he was clearly shielding from Walker and Zeke poked her head around her father's body, and Walker couldn't help but smile.

She looked a hell of a lot like Mary.

"You must be the new client." The man looked him up and down, then Zeke, while three dogs sat at attention as if on some kind of silent command.

Walker had to give himself a little internal shake to find some semblance of who he usually was. He smiled, held out a hand. "Walker Daniels."

"We're doing real names?" Zeke muttered behind him, quiet enough that only Walker heard. When the man turned to Zeke, Zeke did not smile, but he did hold out his hand. "Zeke."

The man shook it and nodded. "Cash Hudson. This is my daughter." He did not offer the daughter's name.

Still, Walker grinned at her. "Hi."

"Hi," she replied with a smile of her own.

This seemed to cause Cash to scowl, but he made a waving motion with his arm. "Come on in then."

Walker shared a look with Zeke, but there was really no other option but to follow the man, and his daughter and dogs, inside.

They were led into the big dining room that was already teeming with people. The huge table was set all fancy like. Some people sat at it, some people stood, all deep in conversation.

That slowly died out as everyone became cognizant of Walker and Zeke standing there. Walker scanned the little crowd for Mary, but she didn't appear to be in the room. Though Carlyle was, and she immediately walked over and crouched in front of the dogs.

They sat obediently while Carlyle petted them and elicited some face licks. The little girl watched Carlyle closely, while the adults all remained quiet.

Until Carlyle wrapped her arms around one of the dogs, clearly in heaven. "Oh, my God. I love them."

"We have lots more," the girl informed her earnestly.

"You, my friend, are living the dream."

The girl beamed at this.

Walker was quite certain silence would have returned after that, but Mary swept in carrying a huge platter. "So, you did decide to come," she greeted cheerfully. She placed the platter on the table and the delicious scents of food quickly filled the room.

Walker was concerned his stomach might rumble. But he forgot all about his stomach when Mary beamed that smile at him. He didn't have the first earthly clue why she took his breath away, only that she did.

"Everyone, that's Walker on the left and Zeke on the right. Now, you come on in and sit and I'll introduce everyone else," Mary said, waving a hand. "Dinner is ready."

There was nothing else to do but find a seat at the table like everyone else was doing. Carlyle had no problem plopping herself right in the middle of things, but Walker and Zeke held back, waiting for the family to take what he presumed were their usual seats before sitting next to each other on one side.

Mary introduced everyone by name, if not relationship. He knew she had four older brothers, and he'd met Cash. The three other brothers weren't hard to pick out— especially the sheriff and the former military one. Of all of the siblings, the only one he might have struggled with was the sister, but since he'd already met her, it was easy to see how she fit. And how the redhead and the black-haired looker didn't really.

But no matter how they were all related, he didn't miss the suspicious glances he and Zeke received.

But there was also just the very normal activity of a family and some strangers settling down to a meal. Everyone passed around plates, and while conversation didn't exactly resume, there was the easy, normal hum of scraping silverware and requests to pass the salt.

"I've been organizing your research," Mary said, serving herself some salad. She seemed to be the last to be handed every plate, and just took whatever was left over. Except for the rolls. She put the last one on the little girl's plate without saying anything. "Anna's been doing some work from the computer side of things. With her and Palmer's expertise, we might be able to dig into some records that you might not have access to. Carlyle was saying that's one area where you guys have struggled."

"It's more an access issue than an area of struggle," Walker responded pleasantly. "But definitely not something we've been able to utilize effectively."

"Well, we have plenty of access to offer," Mary replied. Her smile was pleasant and polite and Walker understood she was offering it to all of them. But it felt like it was for him, and he was really going to need to get his head screwed on straight.

"It'll take a few days to get fully up to speed on your case," Jack said from his spot at the head of the table. He had such a sheriff way about him and Walker tried very hard not to bristle at the authority in his tone. Of course, both his siblings were scowling, so he knew he wasn't the only one.

"But HSS doesn't have any other cases right now to split

our focus. Lots of hands on deck. Mary says you've been investigating yourself for quite a few years."

In a manner of speaking. "Yeah. We worked with the police for the first few." Walker tried to keep the bitterness out of his tone since this guy was the police, but it was hard to maintain the casual smile and relaxed posture. "But there's only so much they can do and for so long."

Jack didn't seem to take offense to that. He nodded. "That's usually where we come in. Mary says this one is dangerous."

Walker nodded. "Someone is definitely out there willing to hurt anyone who exposes the truth. But that's how I know we're on the right track."

"We've got plenty of security here. It's not foolproof. Nothing ever is, but it's safe here, and you're welcome to use everything we have to offer until we get you some answers."

Welcome. It felt like he was being given the king's approval, and Walker was peasant enough to want to thumb his nose at it. He grinned. "Thanks, Sheriff."

Jack's expression cooled a little at that, but then Mary swept in and changed the topic of conversation so that it turned into just a family dinner. It allowed Walker to get a measure of all the Hudsons, something that came easily to him.

Once dinner was over, there was still dessert and lingering conversation. Walker had expected to want to bolt, that it would be a kind of stiff, stifled, uptight affair for rich people.

But there was something easy about all this. A sort of magnified version of the dinners he used to have with his siblings. There was teasing and sarcasm and an easy camaraderie, albeit one likely born of trauma.

But Walker could tell Zeke was chomping at the bit to leave, so once everyone was done with dessert, Walker got up and excused himself so Zeke could follow suit. He asked Carlyle if she really planned to stay up here in a low voice no one else heard.

But she only laughed at him. Walker sighed and he and Zeke left out the door they'd come in. They'd gotten down the porch and maybe a few feet across the yard when Walker heard the door open.

"Walker?"

Walker stopped, turned to see Mary striding across the little porch and toward them.

"I'll leave you to it," Zeke muttered.

"You don't have to…" But Zeke was already walking away. So Walker was standing in the pretty spring evening, watching Mary walk toward him in the moonlight. Something clutched in his chest, so foreign and confusing all he could do was stare as she approached.

Mary frowned at Zeke's quickly disappearing form. "He didn't have to go."

"No, but he seemed to want to."

Her eyes lifted to his. "I'm sorry if that was overwhelming. I'd hoped it might be reassuring."

"It was. I like your family. Even the cop."

She smiled at that. "So do I."

He saw in her expression everything he felt for his own siblings. It ate at him. "I'm not sure you guys understand what kind of target you might be putting on your backs."

Mary took her time responding. He supposed she was thinking over the perfect words to say. She was careful that way. Careful but somehow not afraid of throwing herself into the midst of danger with a virtual stranger, and it was something about that dichotomy that had him way too interested. Too attached.

"We've been targets before. We'll likely be targets again. That's sort of the price to pay for looking for the truth of ugly things." She smiled up at him, if sadly. "It's worth it to try. We know how hard it is to never have the truth."

That sat there in silence for a while, because he didn't know what to say to her. It was hard to believe what she'd been through after sharing a meal with her family. And yet, he understood. It didn't matter how bad life got, all you could do was march on. Find some new normal. Whether you wanted to or not.

Usually not. So why this felt like a want he didn't know. Just that a few days of Mary in his life made him want a new normal where she could turn that prim smile on him.

"Take a walk with me," he said, without thinking it through. Without weighing all the cons of getting mixed up with the woman who was allegedly going to help him solve this decade-old mystery.

She looked back at the house. He didn't think it was so much a consideration of escape as a woman looking back at all her responsibilities and wondering if she could afford to let them go.

"All right."

MARY NEVER STUCK around for cleanup, but it still felt weird leaving her family behind to meander around the property with Walker. Or maybe it felt weird to want to walk around in the dark with a man she barely knew.

Except there was something about Walker that felt like she *did* know him. He had aliases, had lived life chasing a murderer, so no doubt he was a good actor.

She just never felt like he was acting with her. Carlyle? Yes. Zeke didn't put on an act, just froze everyone out.

And in the middle of that was Walker, who wore a mask most definitely. Who was careful when it came to her family. But she felt like she saw behind those walls.

And you are no doubt fooling yourself.

"Your sister clearly loves animals," she offered because it felt like a safe topic to talk about with a man who made her insides jangle like she was made of bells under her skin.

"Yeah, I tried to get her a dog once, but… We just never had the kind of life that made that feasible. Still, we made it work for a few years before he ran off."

It was that, she supposed, that drew her to him. Those offhanded comments about what he'd done for his siblings. What he'd endured. Like it was just what you did. When she knew that there were plenty of people in the world who wouldn't.

"You sure she's okay there in your big house? She can be…" He trailed off and Mary could practically read his thoughts. He didn't want to bad-talk his sister, but he also had concerns about her behavior, just as Carlyle had said.

"I would have hoped dinner tonight would have eased some of your worries. My siblings are a loud, opinionated, not easily offended lot. However Carlyle decides to act, I'm sure we can take it. And I hope you understand that you and Zeke are welcome to join her."

"I know he won't. And I don't think I'd be able to relax."

"Understandable," she said, clasping her hands in front of her as they walked. And she did understand. It would drive her crazy to go to someone else's house and walk around like a guest.

Because you're a control freak.

Well, yes. But that was neither here nor there.

What *was* here, and why she had agreed to walk with him—aside from the very simple reason that she'd wanted to spend time with him alone—was the hope she could convince him to trust Grant or even Jack with the case.

So she didn't have to have the same obnoxious conversation with every member of her family reminding her she'd sworn never to take on another case.

She'd walked him toward the stables without meaning to, but they, like the house, were two places she felt comfortable. In control.

She stopped walking and turned to face him. If she was one of her more fanciful friends—take Chloe, for example—she might have said he looked like a pirate here in the moonlight. All dark features and dangerous glints.

But he was just a man.

And you are just a woman.

She blew out a breath and forced her shoulders back. She could feign bravery. "I feel like I have to say this one more time. I know you trust me, and you want me to lead this case. I understand, to an extent. But now that you've met my family, surely you can see they're just as trustworthy and capable and far more adept at handling cases."

He seemed to think it over—which she appreciated. No jumping to automatic denial. He was listening, and much like after hearing his story about Carlyle and getting her a dog, her heart softened.

And the rest of her softened when he reached out and stroked a finger down her cheek. "I think you're plenty adept."

Her heart was beating overtime, especially when he didn't remove his finger. Just left it there on her jaw like he couldn't quite part with the contact. She swallowed, hoping her voice would come out sounding remotely firm. "At some aspects, yes. Organization and research. Maybe I'll even find something that helps. But I…I tried to lead a case once. Investigate. I put everything into it and I couldn't find an answer."

"You and your brother made it clear answers aren't a guarantee."

"They aren't. And when I'm not involved, I can deal

with that. But when I'm in charge? I can't handle it. It's like softball."

"Well, you've lost me there."

"Failure is part of the game. Sometimes you strike out, no matter how hard you work. I didn't last a season because striking out just *killed* me. I can't…I can't *stand* that kind of routine, accepted failure even when it's just a *game*. When it's a case? It's too important. I want—I need to do everything right."

He studied her, here in the dark. She could hear the faint noises of horses inside the stables, and usually that would offer some comfort, but he was so quiet. His eyebrows drawn together, his expression so serious.

Then he stepped forward and took her hands in his. "One of the lessons I've learned ten years on is that there is no failure. There's only quitting or death. I'm not quitting and I can't control death, so… Nothing is final. Nothing is a failure."

Her heart stuttered over the word *death*, but she supposed he had a point. But it didn't change her point. "I'm not good at it."

"I bet you're not if you gave up after one try."

She couldn't help the little thread of hurt that worked through her. Who was he to agree with her that she wasn't any good at it? But before she could cool her anger and come up with a suitable, polite rejoinder, he kept talking.

"You guys work on it however you need to, okay? But you shouldn't hold yourself back because you're afraid of failing." His fingers moved across her knuckles. "All that does is hold you back from succeeding."

She could only stare at him. It wasn't scolding so much as advice. Passed-along wisdom maybe.

Since she was the one used to doling out both of those things, she didn't know how to react. He seemed to wade through all her carefully erected walls and foundations and poke them at will. So she was on wobbly ground when she was *never* on wobbly ground.

He stepped closer. "I don't want to talk about the case anymore."

"Oh." This strange spark with Walker was way beyond her experience, but she very much understood the way that heated, intense eye contact made her feel. Decidedly wobbly. "W-what do you want to talk about?"

"The fact that I can't seem to stop thinking about kissing you."

"Oh." She had no idea why she didn't have anything smarter to say. Anything seductive or at least witty.

But apparently she didn't need to say anything, because he pulled her close and pressed his lips to hers. Like it was just a normal thing to do. A normal, *necessary* thing to do. Like breathing.

This kiss wasn't like the one at the cabin—all heat and urgency. This was a slow, drugging savor. His hands touched her face, his fingers rough from whatever work he did, but the touch itself gentle too. Until her knees felt like jelly and she simply had to lean into him or melt into the ground.

His hands slid down her back, everything so tender she thought she might cry, and she didn't know why. Or what to do with it. Except kiss him back. Hold on to him.

When he finally pulled away, she looked up at him wondering what he'd done to her. Wondering how something like this happened. And there was this strange, stark, retroactive understanding of some of the things Anna had told her about her relationship with Hawk that hadn't made sense in the moment. That you could *feel* things without knowing why or how. That those feelings might eradicate rational thought.

Though Walker had eased his mouth away from hers, he

still held her close to him. He was looking at her seriously, like he too was confused. Trying to put together the puzzle of whatever this was.

There was only one thing Mary knew for certain. "This probably isn't very professional of me."

Walker threw his head back and laughed, but he didn't let her go. He held her close and Mary... She didn't know what the hell she was doing, and it was scary, sure, but she was discovering that scary didn't make her want to run away.

At least with Walker.

"Just promise me you'll stay involved, all right?" he said softly. And she knew he didn't mean the kiss, he meant the case. She didn't want to make the promise. But how could she not?

She nodded against his shoulder.

He walked her back to the big house. He didn't kiss her again, but he squeezed her hand, then started out in the dark. She worried about him finding the cabin in a place he barely knew, but he seemed so confident. So in control.

And she had the sinking feeling as she went inside that it wouldn't matter how involved or not she was with the case.

If they didn't find him and his family answers, she was going to bear the weight of it for the rest of her life.

Chapter Ten

For the first time in his life, Walker got used to something. It sneaked up on him, day after day. That he had a routine. That he liked learning about the Hudson Ranch. That letting someone into the investigation he'd been running for ten years felt like relief.

Like all these years he'd only needed to stop. Look around the world. Breathe. And things would have been more tenable. More like life and less like a constant race toward and away from danger all at the same time.

He didn't allow himself to dwell on regrets. Or maybe this new world didn't allow it, because how could he regret anything that had led him to Mary?

He wasn't stupid enough to think too deeply about it. He enjoyed each moment as they came. Late-night walks. Kisses in the dark, in the stables, anywhere he could get her alone for a few seconds. He didn't think about feelings, about the future.

It would complicate things.

So he just took it day by day. Eating with the Hudsons, meeting with Mary and whatever sibling had done something for the case that day. Even horse-riding lessons, because Carlyle had desperately wanted to learn, and Walker just wasn't fully comfortable with the amount of time she was spending with Mary. So he'd pretended like he wanted to learn too.

Of course Carlyle was a natural and he was not, and it irritated the hell out of him. So much he'd tried to convince Zeke to join them.

But Zeke refused. Walker knew Zeke did not share this newfound sense of domesticity. That lying low on the Hudson Ranch while they poked at things from computers and combed through old reports they'd been through a hundred times was Zeke's worst nightmare.

The man wanted to act, and Walker understood that. Even if he'd crossed some bridge where what he really wanted was to rest.

So he didn't say anything to Zeke even though he knew his brother was sneaking off doing his own investigations, not letting anyone into what they were—even Carlyle.

Walker could have pushed, but pushing Zeke never got anyone anywhere.

The Daniels siblings and pushing did not go hand in hand.

"Maybe you should give Walker private lessons. He sucks," Carlyle said from where she sat in the saddle of her favorite horse. A gray animal named Robinson.

"Yeah, maybe you should," Walker said, flashing a grin down at Mary, whose cheeks turned a pretty shade of pink.

Carlyle rolled her eyes. "Gross." She swept off the horse in an easy, fluid motion that made Walker scowl. He still couldn't quite manage that effortless movement.

"Your turn, Walker," Mary said pleasantly from where she stood next to her horse, having also dismounted with ease. "Remember. Relax. It's an easy, instinctual move."

Too bad his instincts with horses sucked, as Carlyle said. But he was not a quitter. He used what Mary had taught him over the past few weeks and managed a decent enough dismount, if decidedly not relaxed or easy.

"That's much improved," Mary said, like a kindergarten teacher might to a kid who'd finally mastered writing his name—with backward letters anyway.

Walker grunted and they began the process of leading the horses back into the stables. But Mary's phone chimed and she paused as she pulled it out of her shirt pocket and frowned at the screen. "Anna needs me back at the house."

"She okay?" Walker asked, because he could tell Mary was concerned.

"I'm sure she's fine. She didn't say it was an emergency. Just to come back." Mary tried to smile, but Walker could see the worry around her eyes.

"We've got the horses," Carlyle assured Mary, reaching over to take Mary's reins. "You can always come check to make sure after you're done."

Mary nodded. "All right."

Walker would give her credit, she didn't hesitate. She left, which no doubt made Carlyle feel like Mary thought she could handle it.

However, she did look back over her shoulder once. But Walker liked to think that was about him, not the horses. Because she smiled at him, then shook her head a little and turned back to the house.

The sun tinged her dark hair red as it swung behind her. She moved for the house in long, purposeful strides. All that economical movement should *not* be a turn-on, but everything about her got to him.

He could feel Carlyle studying him so he wrenched his gaze from Mary—and boy did it feel like a wrenching—and turned his attention to tending his horse the way Mary had been teaching him.

At first, they did their work quietly, but eventually Carlyle spoke. "You know, I've never thought I could say this to you before."

"What?" Walker asked, grooming the horse carefully.

Carlyle was silent for a long, stretched-out moment. When she spoke, her voice was soft, uncertain. It reminded him of the time before she'd grown into her personality. When she'd had nightmares and worried someone was out to hurt her—just like they'd hurt their mother.

"We could just…let it go. Not find out. Start life over, and just let it go." She didn't look at him. She stared straight ahead at the horse's flank.

Walker was speechless. He could only stare at her, one hand on his horse and one hand hanging limply at his side. "But someone is after us. I don't think that goes away just because we stop. And you know Zeke won't stop. And we can't just let someone get away with it." He thought better of the way he phrased that, but only after he'd said it. She didn't have to be part of that *we*, not if she didn't want to.

Carlyle nodded, but she kept her head uncharacteristically tipped down. "Yeah."

"Car…"

"No, I get it. And you're right. It's just… This is nice." She focused hard on the task at hand. "It's been a while since we had nice."

Walker couldn't focus on his horse. He could only look at his baby sister, who'd never had a second of normal. He'd always wanted to give it to her, but he supposed as she'd gotten older he'd sort of forgotten. Because she was just so different. So herself. He'd thought she'd been just as wrapped up in finding their mother's killer as he had always been.

But clearly she wasn't. "*You* could. You don't have to be involved."

"Yes, I do," she muttered. Then she smiled at him, but it didn't reach her eyes. And something about the whole exchange stuck with him. Ate at him. He couldn't help feeling like there was something else in play. Something he didn't know.

Something he needed to.

MARY WALKED INTO the house, a mixture of worry and concern cooling all the sunny warmth she'd felt in the little horseback riding lesson with Carlyle and Walker. It was her favorite part of the day.

Well, second favorite. Taking walks around the property with Walker after dinner was her favorite. Because inevitably that led to... She didn't know what to call it exactly. *Making out* sounded so high school. All she knew was that she liked it. It was exciting and fun and didn't come weighed down with questions of what came next. With the responsibilities of adulthood and real life they'd have to face at some point.

She wondered if either one of them would ever push for that next step, or if they were both too afraid. She liked this little routine. It felt like if she didn't push for anything, it could always stay just like this.

Which she knew was foolish. Not to mention, it was not the time to think about it. Her sister had asked her to come back to the house and Mary couldn't fathom a reason that would be good.

She opened the door and stepped inside, not letting her worry get the better of her. "Anna?"

"In the living room."

Mary hurried into the room, where Anna and Hawk sat, hip to hip, on the couch. They were leaning over a computer screen and some pieces of paper were spread out on the coffee table.

When she entered, they moved in a kind of unison that reminded Mary of her parents. Oh, Anna and Hawk were nothing like her parents individually, but something about the way they were with each other spoke of a partnership much longer than the time they'd actually been together. Like they'd been made to fit, just like this. Anna's bump getting bigger, and Hawk's overall health improving every day.

"Palmer finally got his hands on those financial records you wanted," Anna said.

Mary tried not to tense. She hadn't been able to write Walker's father completely off. So many times a woman got murdered it was by a partner or a former partner. Add abuse to the equation, and Mary just figured it was a good line to tug. So, she'd had Palmer look into Don Daniels.

Now, irrationally, she wished she hadn't.

"The cops were right, there's nothing off about his financial situation around the period of the murder, but we looked a lot farther than that," Hawk said.

"There's a pretty hefty deposit in his account—for no discernible reason—six years *after* the murder," Anna said. "Palmer's working on figuring out who paid him, but it's the first real hint we've had to go on."

Because if he'd been inexplicably paid a large sum, even if it was a time later, it was off. A strange circumstance that needed looking into.

She'd have to be the one to tell Walker they needed to look deeper into his father. She doubted he'd be *angry* about that, since he'd been clear that Don had abused him and Zeke.

But still, she didn't want to be the one who had to tell him and taint all the *nice* of the past few weeks. Which was pure cowardice.

She had Anna and Hawk show her the financial records. Not only was there a curious lump sum deposited about six years after Walker's mother's murder, but there were a few smaller ones from the same place, a name that didn't exist, after that.

She went and talked to Palmer about what he was finding on the payer.

"It's very hidden," he said, tapping his fingers next to the computer keyboard. "Which means it's a good thread to follow, but also that I've got to be careful. Which takes time."

Mary nodded.

"I'm also looking into the possibility of aliases for Don Daniels. He mostly disappears about four years ago. No record of death or imprisonment or anything, so I've got to wonder if he's out there under a different name."

A different name. Like Walker used. She tried to just absorb the information. Not jump to conclusions. Not worry about how it would make Walker feel, and what she could do to cushion those feelings.

Palmer studied her. "You okay?"

"Of course."

"You know, when you get personally involved in a case—"

"I don't need lectures, Palmer," she said, with too much snap in her tone, because obviously Palmer would read into that. And be right.

Palmer stood, slipped his arm around her shoulders as he led her out of the small room. "Lectures are not my style, Mary. But getting personally involved in a case just so happens to come under the umbrella of experiences I've had and not done so well at."

She knew he was talking about when he'd helped Louisa solve the mystery of her parentage. "You and Louisa handled it."

"Yeah, we did. But I've done it both ways and getting twisted up in clients makes it harder. Scarier. And more important. So, I'm not lecturing, Mary, I'm saying I understand. And you can always talk to me if you need to."

She leaned into her brother a little bit. She didn't want to talk, but the gesture was nice. Even if taking care and soothing was *her* job.

"I really am fine. I'm just preoccupied with how to tell them. They don't have a great relationship with their father, but I think they'd written him off as a possibility a long time ago."

"He's still only a possibility. Who knows what the money is for. We'll keep digging."

Mary nodded, but she knew the Daniels siblings well enough now to know they wouldn't see it that way. They'd immediately see guilt.

And they'd want to act. Not always wisely. She kept using the word *wild* to describe them, because in essence they *were*. There was no structure. The Hudsons had always had the ranch, Jack's—and to an extent her own—belief that they grow up and go out into the world as productive members of it.

Walker, Zeke and Carlyle had existed in a weird fringe space. The only system or routine they'd ever seemed to have was when Carlyle had been in school.

It was a stark contrast to her own life, one Mary didn't always know how to deal with—no matter how charmed she was by them all. Or how infatuated she was with Walker.

But this case was why they were here. This case was why she knew them. So she could hardly ignore it. Still, she allowed herself a little procrastination. She went to her room and the binder she'd been compiling of all pertinent information and carefully added the new findings.

It was an hour later when she couldn't put it off any longer. She walked out to the ranch hand cabin, binder under her arm, dread creeping in her gut. She tried to assure herself she could be professional no matter how unprofessional she felt toward the man.

She was, after all, excellent at cleaning up after bad news. She was just the person to handle this.

She knocked on the door and waited.

He opened the door, already that big grin on his face. She didn't know what to do with him, with what he made her feel. It was how she imagined being swept out to tide might feel or getting stuck in quicksand. Like she had absolutely no choice against the force of the way his eyes seemed to dance when he grinned at her.

When he kissed her. Which he did now, without saying a word.

She wished so much she could enjoy this moment, sink into the kiss and him. Wished they could forget why he'd been here the last few weeks and just keep pretending this was normal.

"Zeke is off doing what Zeke does," he said, pulling her inside. "Carlyle conned Cash into letting her help with dog training, which means you and I are alone." He grinned at her, then kissed her again.

She wanted to cry, and that was so foolish. Whatever was going on between her and Walker was clearly a kind of fling. She didn't know how to navigate that, but she knew he was very careful to keep things light. Casual.

Which was fine. She'd never had light and casual in her life. Why not have it with the man who was just stopping through? A fling. A moment in time. Something to look back fondly on.

But the binder was still under her arm and no matter how good it felt to kiss Walker, to have his hands on her, the corner of the binder dug into her arm like a sharp reminder of why they knew each other in the first place.

She managed to pull her mouth away from his, though she was a little breathless. "Walker..."

Something stopped him then. The tone of her voice, the

look on her face, she didn't know. He studied her carefully, that grin slowly morphing into something far more guarded.

"You found something," he said. And shock was clearly etched across his face, though he tried to wipe it off. "You found something," he repeated. Then he nodded, taking a breath. "All right. Lay it on me."

But he didn't let her go, and Mary decided to hold on to that.

Chapter Eleven

Walker figured it was an effective enough cold shower. Mary was clearly in some kind of emotional turmoil over what she'd found.

She hesitated, then moved out of the circle of his arms, pulling a binder he hadn't even noticed from under her arm. "It's just a potential something, not a full-on something, but it involves your father."

"We already looked into my father."

"I know, but sometimes in cold cases you have to go over things that have already been done." She moved over to the little table, setting the binder down and opening to one of the back pages. "It's not that what you've looked into is wrong, just that it might lead to new avenues."

He didn't know why, but the idea of new avenues pissed him off. Still, he tried to keep that reaction out of his tone. "If it's him, that's great. But—"

She looked up, her eyebrows drawing together. "You're already dismissing the idea."

He didn't know what to say to that because, hell yeah he was dismissing it.

"You haven't even listened to what we found."

"I just don't think he did it, Mary. I wish I did. But I know the guy. He's not smart enough for some kind of ten-year conspiracy."

She didn't say anything for a few moments. She was just utterly still. "You hired me to look into this. Insisted I did. Now you won't even to listen to what we found?"

"I'll listen. I'm just saying, we've been down this road. I get why you guys might think it's *the* road, but it's not."

Something flashed in her expression. Not quite anger, but something like it. She closed the binder very carefully. "All right. Well, I'm sorry for bothering you then." She turned, as if to leave, and Walker was dumbfounded.

He stepped in her way before he'd fully thought the move through. Just that her leaving with that blank expression on her face was unbearable. "I don't understand why you're mad. I said I'll listen."

"But you don't *want* to listen."

"So what? Life is just full of what we want? Not my life."

"Not mine, either, Walker."

"I didn't say—" He raked his hands through his hair. What the hell were they doing? He didn't have the vaguest idea why they were arguing, why she was mad. Which was his first clue that this wasn't actually about him. The root cause was hers.

Then he remembered her softball analogy, and the failure comment. The way she said she wasn't any good at it—because getting it wrong messed with her head.

"Honey. This isn't…" He didn't know how to say it. What the right words were. It flirted with something more serious than he could afford. And she and this place all conspired against him to make him believe he could.

"This is why it isn't smart to blur lines," she said coolly.

"I like all the blurred lines just fine." He tried out a grin.

It clearly didn't land. Her eyes narrowed.

"So, you think I'm so incapable, you'd rather talk me into bed, then—"

"Talk you into bed? Are you kidding me?" It poked at his

own temper because didn't he wish it was just about talking
her into bed. "It's been weeks and we're sneaking around
like teenagers. Because I can't stop thinking about you. Because I want to be where you are. Because something about
you makes my lungs feel like they've been tied in knots.
When I'm with you, I don't think about my damn goal in
life. I think about you. About us. So yeah, sorry if I'd pick
that over dealing with all the shit and ugliness of my past."

He felt like an idiot, and still he couldn't walk away. He
reached out, fitted his palm to her cheek. "I don't want to
argue with you, Mary."

She closed her eyes and blew out a breath. "My fault,"
she said. "I just…" She sucked in a breath that must have
been fortifying because she opened her eyes and met his
gaze. "I'm really not good at people telling me I'm doing
something wrong."

He laughed, couldn't help it. Damn, why did he like her
so much?

"Show me what you found. It's not about being wrong.
It's about ripping a scab off an old wound. Who wants to
do that? But if it has to be done, it has to be done." Because
more and more he wanted an end to this.

It wasn't so much about finding answers anymore. It was
about building the life that came next.

She swallowed, looked down at the binder, and he could
see the tug-of-war playing out all over her face. He supposed that was a kind of progress, that she wasn't trying to
hide that from him.

She cleared her throat. "We looked into your father's financial situation."

"Yeah, the cops did that too."

"For a specific period of time. We looked for longer."
She took a deep breath. He noticed that her face was very
carefully arranged in that neutral expression he didn't care

for, but her hand shook a little as she pointed to the page she'd just opened up to. "A lump sum. Six years after the murder, deposited into his bank account."

He frowned, because that *was* new. He knew Zeke kept an eye on their father, but he hadn't mentioned this. And what would have prompted them to look into his finances when he was basically a nomad?

So he looked at the page, the list of deposits. The large one and the date. And his blood went cold. Because it wasn't just six years after the murder.

"That's Carlyle's birthday."

Mary whipped her head to look up at him. "What?"

"July fourteenth. That's her birthday." He didn't even need to do the math to realize it. "And that year? That was her eighteenth birthday."

Mary shook her head and looked up at him with big, sympathetic eyes. "Walker, I don't know how that could be a coincidence."

"I don't either." It was hard to get his breath because this was hardly all. It was just the tip of the iceberg. "Mary, our apartment complex burned down on that day. We got out, and no one ever thought it had anything to do with us." He was seeing little spots. "Carlyle did."

"Come on. Let's sit down." She took his hand and led him over to the lone chair. She nudged him until he kind of collapsed onto it.

The whole thing at the stables kept playing in his mind. That Carlyle wanted to let it go but he couldn't. He thought it was devotion to their mother. She didn't remember the things he did.

But what if it was something else?

"She's acting weird. I keep trying to tell myself it's just she doesn't know how to stick in one place. Or trust people to help. But this…"

"Is it possible she knows something she hasn't told you or Zeke?"

It crushed him. Because he didn't know how it *wasn't* possible now.

MARY COULD ONLY stand next to the chair and watch Walker deal with this new set of facts. She felt like an idiot for over-reacting earlier. For making his tragedy about *her* issues.

This wasn't about her. So she brushed her hand over his hair as he sat there, elbow on his knees, hands curled in his wild, dark hair. She could imagine what he was feeling. Trying to wade through all the reasons Carlyle might have kept something from him.

She'd had a hand in creating this problem, so she needed to fix it. "Why don't I go track her down? I'll bring her back here and you two can talk."

Walker laughed. Bitterly. "Talk. And say what? Demand answers? That's not how you get through to Carlyle."

"Why don't you show her what I showed you? See what she has to say."

Walker shook his head. "If she wanted to tell me, she would have by now."

Mary tried not to sigh. Men could be so stubborn. Particularly when it came to their sisters, as she knew firsthand. "Maybe, Walker. But maybe she's afraid. Or protecting you. She *is* the one who contacted HSS originally. There could be an understandable reason behind this."

"Yeah. They'll all piss me off."

She kissed the top of his head because it felt like the right thing to do. "Probably. But they're still answers. And forward movement."

He grunted, clearly stewing over the fact that Carlyle hadn't told him something, rather than focusing on the fact that they now had this new lead to tug on. The information about Carlyle's birthday and their apartment fire and the hefty deposit didn't tell them anything—except that they had to be connected.

They just had to be.

"If you don't want to, why don't I talk with her?" Mary suggested. "I'm very good at getting information out of people."

He shifted so he could study her, somewhat skeptically. "Are you?"

"I got your real name out of you in under an hour."

His mouth curved, not quite that grin she'd wanted, but a smile nonetheless. "So you did."

"People see a calm, dowdy demeanor—"

"I have never once thought of you as dowdy." As if to prove his point, he pulled her onto his lap. It should have felt ridiculous, but instead felt kind of nice to have his arms around her, to have him close.

Like they were in this together.

"The point is, people tend to underestimate me. Because I don't have a temper—"

"You don't let your temper loose *angrily*. You just get all frosty. But that's still temper," he interrupted. "It's just not the one people are expecting."

She resisted a groan at his constant interruptions. "I can be very persistent, but I know how to gentle it so people don't know I'm being persistent. So they feel like they want to tell me, rather than get all defensive."

"You're a fluffy steamroller."

"You wouldn't be the first to call me that."

"Danielses are just flat-out steamrollers, Mary."

"Yes, well, fluffy steamrollers are flexible. And they might get flattened, but they pop right back up."

"This is the weirdest analogy." He blew out a long breath, his arms tightening their hold around her. "It'd probably be better coming from you. It'll feel like an unbiased voice. I'll end up yelling."

She could picture him angry. She'd seen him run away from men with guns with an immense amount of calm, but underneath that had been a sharp-edged anger. She'd seen it flash in his eyes a couple of times.

But no matter how she tried, she could not picture him losing his temper with Carlyle. "I don't think you're the stern taskmaster you think you are."

He pulled a face. "Well, now you just sound like Zeke."

Yes, she could picture the stiff, stern younger brother yelling. It was strange, that though a similar thing had happened to the Daniels siblings when they'd lost their parents and then had to take care of one another, the dynamics had settled differently. Walker might be the oldest, but he had a softness to him she hadn't seen out of Zeke.

She wrapped her arms tighter around him, settled easier into his lap, into this little cocoon of warmth. His shoulders were tense, but they relaxed a little when she did.

"I feel like it's all about to crash," he said, shaking his head a little. "After all these years juggling balls, they're all about to fall."

Her heart ached for him. Because she knew what it was like to worry about that kind of thing. The strength it took to keep taking care of everyone even when you felt that way. "Balls bounce."

"Important ones shatter," he returned flatly.

She pressed a kiss to his temple, couldn't resist the urge to soothe him. "Carlyle won't shatter. She has you and Zeke. All three of you have each other. It's what's gotten you this far, and it's what will get you through figuring out what this all means."

He took her hand in his, ran his thumb over her knuckles.

"This is usually the part where I throw myself into something dangerous and impulsive."

Her heart ached for the young man he must have been, and all he'd had to deal with. She knew, firsthand, what that kind of weight did to you. The ways coping mechanisms helped you cope but didn't always help you thrive.

Her issues with control might be twisted up in everything she couldn't.

She had to clear her throat to speak. Because control or not, she wanted to help him. Soothe him. Fix this. "Well, let's sidestep that for now. I'll talk to Carlyle, and we'll go from there."

He looked up at her then, those dark eyes meeting hers and searching for something. She didn't know what, but it made her heart beat in triple time.

"I've never wanted to know what comes next," he said, seriously. "Never thought about the future. It's only ever been about answers—and usually for Carlyle and Zeke. Not me. Not my mother. I think if it had just been me, I would have been happy not knowing. Happy to leave it all behind. But I didn't have a clue what I'd do if I did. This is all I've had since I was twenty years old."

The air was clogging her lungs, but she forced herself to speak carefully. Neutrally. "What were you doing? College?"

He snorted, but it wasn't exactly a bitter sound. "I barely survived high school. Sitting still in a classroom for hours on end is not for me. Even if it had been an option, I wouldn't have put myself through that nightmare. I considered the military, but eventually I just went to trade school. Now, don't laugh, but the idea was to become an electrician."

"Why would I laugh at that?"

"I don't know. It seems very uncool when compared with saying I spent ten years tracking my mother's murderer and

avoiding certain death. Though, in fairness, cooler than saying I worked in the school cafeteria to keep my little sister
in line."

It surprised a little laugh out of her. She supposed that
was a big piece of why she couldn't help but like him so
much. He surprised her, and it never felt bad. No matter
how she didn't know how to deal with it, she wanted more
of those surprises.

"I'd like to know what comes next. What happens after.
Know that Zeke and Carlyle are good and maybe I can have
that life other people get to have."

She wanted to cry for him, wade in and fix it for him,
but she couldn't think of a way to do that. Except to start
by talking to Carlyle. "You should have that, Walker. Everyone should."

He studied her hand in his again. She couldn't read his
expression. It was as serious, as focused as he'd been in that
first moment she'd met him when he'd been clearly preparing for whoever was after him.

And is after him still, or will be. She didn't let that thought
take root. She didn't want to be afraid. Not in this little
pocket of warmth. She'd been through too many bad times
not to believe in enjoying the bits and pieces of good that
came along with them.

"And would you be in it?" he asked, his voice quiet but
firm. He didn't meet her gaze, but she couldn't call it nerves
or hesitation. It was something else, and it had more to do
with how weighty this all was.

How important.

This was a turning point for them. Walker didn't fit into
her ordered world. Not the reality of it. These last few weeks
had been like a bubble, away from reality.

Choosing him, accepting the idea of some sort of "after,"

would mean change. Losing some of that control she'd had a death grip on since she'd been ten years old.

And in this moment, looking into his dark eyes as he studied her, waiting patiently for an answer, control seemed like the last thing she'd want to hold on to if it meant losing him. So she leaned forward and pressed her mouth to his. "I'd like to be," she murmured against his lips.

His grip tightened, taking the kiss deeper, until it seemed it was all that mattered. All that would ever be.

"Come to bed with me, Mary. Let's put this all away, just for a little while."

And she knew, if she wanted to later, she'd be able to convince herself she was just trying to make him feel better. That it had been about soothing him because she was good at that.

But she went to the bedroom with him because she *wanted* to. Because something deep and meaningful twined them together, and it didn't matter what was going on around them.

As long as they could enjoy each other.

Chapter Twelve

Walker dozed. He wasn't a man for afternoon naps, but with Mary cuddled next to him, satisfaction warming his blood and his bed, why not catch a few winks? Why not lie here and feel the steady rise and fall of Mary's breathing? It was the first place he'd ever been in his life where things seemed to make sense.

But before he could fully relax into sleep, he heard the telltale sound of the front door creaking open out there in the cabin. He winced. It would no doubt be Zeke, and it'd be hard to hide what he and Mary had been up to.

She shot up into a sitting position, pulling the sheet with her. "Is that Zeke?" she asked in a hissed whisper.

"Probably."

She practically leaped out of bed, frantically searching for her clothes and putting them on so haphazardly and with such panic, he could only watch in amusement.

"I'm not sure I've ever seen you move so fast."

She glared at him, pants and bra on, but one sock missing and no shirt. Her hair was disheveled. She looked more rumpled than she had when they'd been on the run from gunmen.

She really was something. He crossed his arms behind his head and grinned at her.

"How are we going to explain this?" she whispered.

Walker shrugged from his comfortable and enjoyable position on the bed. "Zeke knows I'm not a monk."

She paused, just for a second, then found her shirt and pulled it on—less haphazard, more stiff. "Just how much of a not-monk are you?" she asked primly.

He grinned at her, though she had her back to him as she pulled her shirt into place. "Do I sense jealousy, Mary?"

Her back stiffened and she turned to face him with that cool, regal expression. "No. Of course not."

He got out of bed, didn't bother to grab his boxers just yet. Her cool expression didn't falter, but her cheeks turned pink and her eyes definitely dropped. "Because monk or not, it was all before you."

"Yes, exactly." Her chin went up in the air. "That's why I couldn't care less."

God, she was amazing. He pulled on his boxers, then crossed the room to her. Touched his finger to that silky jaw. "None of them mattered," he whispered into her ear, before pressing a kiss just beneath her earlobe.

Her exhale was shaky, but her words were firm. "Oh, now, I don't need charming words and pretty lies. It hardly matters—"

"Not a lie. Wish it was." Because that would make this simple, but it only seemed to get more complicated with every step. And he didn't just mean her. But she was the reason all the fear and frustration and discomfort seemed infinitely worth it. "You make everyone and everything fade away."

She let out a little shuddery breath. "I don't know how to be when you say things like that."

He knew he'd almost distracted her enough from Zeke's arrival, but the jerk kept making noise out there and she shook her head and pulled herself together.

"Well, Mary, it's probably about time you didn't know

how to be. Now come on. You're helping me explain this whole thing with my father to Zeke. He'll have all sorts of questions I didn't." Because Walker never wanted to ask questions when it came to his father. He'd spent years blaming his mother's murder on Don Daniels—with no proof, and in fact quite a bit of proof to the contrary.

It hadn't mattered. Don was an easy target. Walker had wanted it to be him so all that hate just stayed in one damn place.

But he'd never been able to get anywhere near proving it, and even Zeke had told him they needed to move on years ago. Now Mary was reintroducing the possibility—with not proof exactly, but possibility—and Walker...

Well, he wanted to run away from it. Because those were his two MOs. Impulsively throwing himself into danger or turning away from it altogether.

Mary had introduced some kind of weird middle ground where his instinct was to do both, and yet he knew he couldn't do either.

Most alarming and unsettling of all was that it didn't seem to matter. Because Mary was here, with her implacable steadiness and her hand in his.

"You need to put on clothes, Walker," she said, and her tone was a mix of gentle reminder and stern schoolteacher. Was it any wonder he was halfway in love with her? No one had ever stepped in and talked him down from a ledge. Zeke or Carlyle might have tried, but he'd never listened.

But Mary... She'd sat there with him, talked him through, and suggested he sidestep the whole diving headfirst into danger. She'd comforted him, and it hadn't occurred to him not to let her.

He smoothed a hand over her tangled hair. "You might want to fix this mess."

She reached up and patted her hair. "Oh," she said with some distress. "Do you have a brush?"

"There's a comb in the bathroom."

She frowned. "I'd have to go out there to get to the bathroom."

"That you would."

She fisted her hands on her hips, all scolding censure. "Walker."

"Come on, Mary. I'm guessing Zeke's figured it out. But luckily it's Zeke and not Carlyle, so he won't say anything. In front of you anyway."

MARY HAD NEVER felt more off-kilter in her whole entire life. She'd just had sex—fantastic, mind-blowing sex in fact, which was definitely a first as her college experience had been less than stellar—and then Walker had said all those sweet things in that matter-of-fact way he had that made it hard not to believe them. Harder still to remain ordered and calm.

Now he wanted her to just walk into the living room where his brother was and talk about the case? When her heart was still thundering and her knees felt a little weak? When Zeke would absolutely know what had just gone on in that bedroom? Mary wasn't ashamed. She'd likely go home and tell Anna all about it.

But who wanted to face their partner's brother in the midst of the after-good-sex glow?

Walker was pulling her along, though, and what else was there to do? She wasn't going to cower and hide in the bedroom and find some way to sneak out. That felt wrong.

More wrong than facing this awkwardness.

She lived with siblings who were in committed relationships and quite obviously had sex in the privacy of their own rooms. They never acted awkward.

Well, Grant and Dahlia sometimes did. But they were more introverted. And Mary, well, she supposed she was too. But the point was it certainly hadn't stopped them.

Zeke was standing in the little kitchenette. He was making coffee and the way he was setting things down hard and closing drawers loudly when he usually moved like some kind of feline predator made Mary realize all the noise had been for their benefit. Walker just squeezed her hand.

"Hey, glad you're back. We've got something of a lead," Walker announced.

"Is that what we're calling it these days?" Zeke muttered, with his back to them and so quietly Mary almost didn't catch it.

She in fact wished she hadn't.

But he turned and his expression was unreadable. "All right. Let's hear it."

Walker dropped her hand and went over to her binder. He explained the financial records and handed them over to Zeke, who studied them in broody silence.

"Who's the one paying him?"

"Palmer is digging into that," Mary explained, "but since we know there have been threats against you guys, he has to be careful. Which takes time."

Zeke nodded.

"Did you notice the date?" Walker prompted.

"Yeah, I noticed."

"I think she knows something."

Zeke's expression didn't really change, but Mary sensed a darker mood all the same.

"I'll talk to her," he said. And Mary couldn't hide the wince. She definitely wouldn't want to be Carlyle if Zeke was going to talk to her in this mood.

"I think we need to try an alternative route to answers," Walker said, and she recognized the attempt at peace. She was usually the one accomplishing peace in her family. It was a little surprising to see Walker do it. She'd just supposed they never had peace—went about every family discussion in their wild, lawless way. "Mary could talk to her. Maybe she'd open up to someone else. Someone she didn't feel the need to protect."

Zeke's dark gaze turned to her, hard and cold. Mary smiled kindly in return, though it was difficult to maintain under that mean stare.

"She's not going to listen to us," Walker continued. "We know this. We've been down this road a hundred times with a hundred things. She'll shut down or worse."

"But she'll listen to a stranger?"

She saw the flash of anger on Walker's face on her behalf so she stepped between the brothers and spoke before Walker could.

"I understand why you'd think that, Zeke. I see this from your point of view, but maybe you should see it from Carlyle's. She doesn't see me as a stranger because she's engaged with me and my family the past few weeks. She hasn't made herself scarce or refused to be drawn into conversation." Maybe scolding wasn't the way to go, but it was only the truth.

Zeke's scowl got deeper and deeper. But he didn't argue with her.

"What's more, sometimes a stranger is better. You're her two older brothers, who've protected her for the majority of her life. Or tried to. She likely feels a responsibility to you—whether not to upset you, or to protect you, or something else. She has none of those things when it comes to me. I'm just part of the family she hired in hopes of some answers. And maybe, if you two hadn't gotten involved, she would have told us these things earlier."

Zeke crossed his arms over his chest. "So it's our fault?"

"There's no fault when it comes to how you deal with tragedy. Everyone's doing their best. I know that's hard to see sometimes in the middle of it, but whatever Carlyle knows, or doesn't, she's doing her best too."

She looked back at Walker, and she couldn't quite read his expression, but she knew the words resonated with him too. Because she knew he blamed himself for things. That's why he tended to choose rash or impulsive methods of dealing with situations. It was better to do that than marinate in guilt. But when it came to tragedy, raising and protecting your siblings, guilt was just a cornerstone of it all. She understood that, and he'd likely never had anyone in his life who did.

She hadn't outside of her family.

It made her feel a wave of warmth and care and other things she couldn't pick apart and analyze in this little cabin with two complicated men and one frustrating mystery.

"I'll go talk to her. If she tells me anything, I'll encourage her to tell you both herself. If she doesn't, I'll let you know and we can look at our options. In the meantime, Palmer will be researching where the money came from, and I'm going to start looking into the apartment fire. And maybe while I do that, you could discuss with Walker whatever it is that you've been doing."

Zeke's expression grew cold again. "Excuse me?"

"It doesn't escape my notice you're not here. So you must be somewhere doing something. Walker is content to let you do it, and maybe I should be too. It's none of my business after all, what with me being a stranger. But if I wanted to solve a mystery, I'd stop being secretive and start working together." She delivered it all with her cool, older-sister voice and a pleasant smile. She ended that little speech with, "I'll see you both at dinner." Not a question.

A command.

Then Mary turned on a heel and walked, head held high, out the door. She didn't know Zeke well enough to know if that little speech would be effective, but she liked to think it would be.

Either way, she knew she was right. And that was all that mattered. She was down the porch stairs before the door opened behind her.

"Wait a sec," Walker called.

She turned and watched him approach. He didn't say anything, though, just pulled her into his arms and pressed his mouth to hers. He kissed her, clearly not caring at all if Zeke was watching, and that helped her not care too. Because this wasn't about the case. It was about them. They'd found each other in the midst of the case and they certainly didn't need anyone's approval.

"You are something else, Mary Hudson." And he grinned down at her, like to him she really was.

It scared her how much she wanted to be.

And how much failure was waiting if she couldn't be.

Still she smiled at him, straightened her shirt that he'd rumpled. "If you're not opposed, you could spend the night in the big house tonight."

"Is that an invitation to your bed?"

She had never in a million years thought she might invite someone, let alone someone like Walker, to share her bed in her family home, but… "Yes, it is."

"Then I'll be there."

Chapter Thirteen

Mary walked back to the ranch focused on Carlyle. She practiced what she'd say to the woman and tried to focus on process over results.

Mary liked to believe that a lifetime with Anna meant she knew how to get through contrary natures. A lifetime with Jack and Grant meant an incredible amount of experience fighting against stubborn hardheadedness. And being herself meant she understood the strange and complex role of being a woman in the midst of men who thought they had to handle everything.

She liked to believe she was especially equipped to get through to Carlyle and get the necessary information, but...

Well, what if she couldn't?

She slowed her pace as she walked to the stables. She didn't know where Carlyle would be, but if she had to guess it'd be with the horses or with Cash's dogs.

The thought of having to face Walker at dinner with no answers, with only failure, twisted her gut into knots. She was flirting with disaster here, and now it wasn't just her own. It was failing Walker, who she...

She...

She couldn't really love him, no matter how her heart seemed to think that was the case. Maybe she'd gotten to know him these past few weeks, but that wasn't enough to love him.

She tried to ignore all the times Anna insisted she'd fallen in love with Hawk at first sight. Mary was too practical to believe in such a thing. Love required a foundation.

And this was not about love. It was about murder.

She reminded her brain of this over and over and once she finally found Carlyle—throwing a rope bone to one of Cash's dogs behind the dog pen—it wasn't so hard to switch focus.

Carlyle threw the rope with a great heave that had Copper the dog yipping with delight as he zoomed after it. Mary came to stand next to Carlyle.

"You know you live in just about the coolest place, right?" Carlyle said by way of greeting. She was tracking the dog's movements as she spoke.

Mary smiled in spite of all her turmoil. Because she did in fact know that, and she was glad Carlyle appreciated it.

"Yes, we do. I hope this isn't jumping any kind of gun, but whenever this is over, I'd certainly be able to find you a place here."

"What do you mean?" Carlyle turned to her for a moment, and the happy enjoyment in her expression had turned wary. Suspicious.

Mary felt instant sympathy for the Daniels clan. Clearly they'd had so few people to trust. "Well, we always need help around the ranch. We're in the process of hiring a ranch hand and we might promote someone, which would open up an entry-level position. I've also been trying to convince Cash to hire an assistant. Then there's Sunrise itself, where I could help you find a job. If you're looking to stay, that is."

"Because you have a thing for my brother and you want *him* to stay?"

Mary didn't sigh at the skepticism, though she wanted

to. "I do have a thing for your brother," she replied, because there was no point lying about it. That would only discredit her. "But this offer doesn't have anything to do with him. I'd offer it to all three of you because I know how lucky I am and have been to have this as home base. Everyone deserves a home base."

Carlyle crouched as Copper returned with the bone. She did a little tug-of-war with the dog, before giving him the order to drop, which he did dutifully. She threw it again.

"Well, I guess we have to figure out this stuff first," she finally said, still watching the dog.

"Yes, we do," Mary agreed. "But we're getting somewhere with that."

"Oh, yeah?"

"We did some digging into your father's finances." Mary watched Carlyle's face carefully. There was no change, but Mary thought she sensed a stiffness. "He received a lump-sum payment from a mysterious source about six years after the murder."

"Huh. Well, that's weird, but he's a shady guy so who knows what shady things he was up to."

An interesting take, and as Walker had a much stronger reaction to it, Mary could only find herself even more suspicious of what Carlyle knew. Still, she kept her tone light. Completely benign.

"The deposit happened on July fourteenth." There was no reaction from Carlyle, but she was staring pretty hard at the dog. "Walker said that's your birthday."

Carlyle crouched as Copper returned. She kept her head down as she tugged on the bone. "Yeah."

"Six years after would have been your eighteenth birthday, to be precise."

"Huh."

"Walker also said your apartment complex burned down that day, and you thought it was connected to the murder."

Carlyle stood abruptly, heaved the rope bone. She turned to face Mary and her expression had gone a little belliger- ent. "Yeah, I was pretty paranoid back then. I'm not fol- lowing how this has anything to do with the case. Walker and Zeke ruled Don out of the equation a long time ago."

Mary studied the young woman's lifted chin, flashing eyes and wanted to engulf her in a hug. She wanted to soothe that restless, hurting soul. But she knew it wouldn't be wel- comed, so she only smiled softly.

"Carlyle," she said. "We can't help if you're keeping se- crets. My family can't and your brothers can't. And we all want to help."

Carlyle's expression changed, almost imperceptibly, from all that anger and what Mary thought was probably fear, to something icier. But the woman smiled politely. "I don't know what you're talking about, Mary. You have all the information I do."

But it was a lie. Mary knew it. "Okay. Maybe we're just missing something. What can you tell me about your fa- ther?"

"Nothing. Because we got out of there before I remem- ber anything about the guy." She crouched, immediately told the dog to drop it this time.

"You never met him? Never heard your mother talk about him?"

"Why are you interrogating me?" Carlyle demanded, standing with the rope bone still in her hand. "That's not how this is supposed to go."

"You started this. Last year you tried to hire us under Walker's alias."

"Yeah, because I thought maybe you guys could pro- tect him."

An interesting way to phrase it. Not about answers, but about…protecting. Mary filed that information away. "But not you?"

"What do you want from me, Mary?" Carlyle said, frustration and anger clearly bubbling over. "Answers I don't have? Okay, so my dad got paid on my eighteenth birthday. Six years after my mom died. The day our apartment complex burned down. What am I supposed to think about that?"

"I don't know, but I'd like to."

"You're supposed to be the one with answers. Your grand HSS."

"And maybe we could find them if we had the whole picture," Mary continued calmly, never letting any kind of emotion show. Because it seemed to be getting under Carlyle's skin and Mary figured that was the best way to get answers. It was how she always succeeded.

And if you don't…

Carlyle heaved the rope. "Find them your damn self." Then she stalked away from Mary—not toward the big house or even the ranch hand's cabin. Mary wasn't sure where she was going, but she knew that this was a big fat failure.

She tried to remember what Walker had said about failure. That giving up was the failure, but this felt pretty bad. She'd have to tell him Carlyle hadn't given her anything, after all her grand talk about being so persuasive and the right person to talk to Carlyle. All she'd done was make Carlyle mad.

Copper returned, nudged her leg with the rope bone. Mary swallowed back the tears. She wouldn't cry. She would try to take a page out of Walker's book and just not give up.

But how?

ZEKE HADN'T SAID MUCH. He'd spent an inordinate amount of time with his nose buried in Mary's binder. Walker had gotten more and more stir-crazy, but he didn't know what to do with himself.

His impulse was to find a flight to California and track down dear old Dad and demand answers. A month ago, that's exactly what he would have done.

Somehow, everything had changed.

Zeke finally closed the binder, then glanced at the clock on the oven. "Guess we should head up to the big house for dinner."

Walker studied his brother. *"We?"* Zeke had been keeping scarce, living off whatever leftovers Mary shoved into the refrigerator when he wasn't looking.

Zeke shrugged. "I want to know if Mary got through to Car or not."

Which felt like pressure. And Walker knew how much pressure Mary put on herself. How afraid of failure she was. He couldn't let Zeke make that worse. "Even if she didn't—"

"I thought you were so confident it was the right course of action."

"I am. It is. But Carlyle's tough and if she has a secret she's been keeping for many years, then you can't be hard on Mary. She's doing her best."

"Is she? Or is she sleeping with you?"

Walker had fought with his brother a lot. As kids. As adults. Sometimes, when they'd been younger, they'd even traded punches. Life had been hard, and sometimes when it was, you took it out on the people you knew would be there no matter what.

But Zeke talking about Mary like that made him angrier than he'd been in a long time. Since he hadn't spent any time with Zeke in so long, he worked to keep his temper in check rather than throw the first punch. "You don't have to like it. You don't have to approve of it. But I care about her, so you'll watch what you say."

Zeke's expression didn't change, but he didn't offer any more commentary. Just nodded, once.

"Good," Walker muttered and turned on a heel, feeling like a hundred different kinds of idiot. Care about her. It sounded so stupid. He tried to walk off the irritating, confusing feelings rattling around inside him as they headed over to the big house, but he didn't succeed.

This was such a habit by now, though, that he didn't feel weird about walking right in the house anymore. It just felt like what you did. He'd walk in and everyone would be getting the table set up, and Carlyle would be elbow to elbow with Izzy playing with the dogs, and then Mary would sweep in and maybe something in him would settle.

It usually did.

But the air was different, he could tell that immediately. Anna came out of the kitchen. "Well, she's not there." Anna looked over at him. "And she's not with you, apparently."

"Mary? No, she came back ages ago."

"Dinner's all ready, but I don't know where she went."

Walker couldn't help but glance over at Carlyle. His baby sister currently had her head bent over a dog, clearly hiding her face. It didn't take a genius to put together what had happened.

"She must be up in her room. I'll go get her," Anna said.

"You mind if I do? I've got something I want to talk to her privately about." He kept his gaze on Carlyle, hoping she'd look up so he could glare disapprovingly at her.

She didn't.

"Uh. Okay. I guess," Anna said, clearly not fully okay with that. "Upstairs. The first door to the left."

Walker nodded, then went to the stairs. He'd spent a lot of time in this house over the past few weeks, but never had cause to venture upstairs. So this felt strange, and wrong. But if Mary was deviating from her schedule, Walker just knew it couldn't be good.

The first door on the left was closed so he lifted his hand and knocked.

"Oh. Just…just a minute," Mary's voice came from inside.

But there was something about the tone that didn't sound right. Maybe it was wrong, but he hadn't grown up in a nice, big house learning manners. A Daniels barged in. So, that's what he did.

She was sitting on the edge of her bed, some little box next to her. She wiped her cheeks quickly, clearly trying to hide the evidence that she'd been crying, but she was still crying, so it didn't work.

"What's wrong?"

"Oh, Walker. What are you doing up here?" Her hands fluttered around, which was when he noticed a bandage and realized the box next to her was a . "I'm sorry. I'm late for dinner. I just burnt my hand." She held up her hand.

"That's why you're crying?"

She straightened her shoulders, clearly trying to get a hold of herself. And not quite getting there.

"Of course," she said firmly. So firmly it sounded like a lie. "It hurt."

Walker crossed the space between them, moved the first-aid kit out of the way, then took a seat. He grabbed her hand, studied the bandage. "Should you see a doctor?"

She shook her head vehemently. "It might blister, but it's fine." The word *fine* seemed to get stuck in her throat and more tears began to fall.

This was clearly not about the burn. "What did Carlyle say? She never learned any manners, and that's my fault. So, blame me. Be mad at me. Just don't cry." He brushed tears away with his thumbs as something painful twisted deep in his gut. He couldn't stand it, her being sad.

"It isn't your fault. It's mine. I thought I could get through to her, and I didn't. Which is fine. I mean, it isn't fine, but it… I just… I was fine, and then I didn't have enough onions."

"Okay." He had no idea why they were suddenly talking about onions, but he'd dealt with enough upset people to know you just rolled with it until you found the thread.

"I had the meal all planned out. I should have had enough onions, but then I didn't and I had to do everything on the fly. And then I burnt my hand." She sniffled.

"Well, if it makes you feel better, if I had to cook for a million people I'd be burning my hand every day."

But she didn't laugh like he'd hoped. She just kept frowning at the floor. And the tears kept coming.

"Everyone thinks I'm so with it, but I'm just a mess. I used to be able to hide it better. It's why I don't get involved. It's why…"

"Hey." He lifted her chin until she met his gaze. He wasn't sure where this had all come from, except he knew something about breaking points. Maybe he didn't get why onions might have set her off, but he knew it didn't always have to connect.

And he understood her. He really did. "Nothing that happens with Carlyle or this case is something I'm going to blame you for. You not having immediate success with my wildling of a sister? Not even close to blaming you for."

"Only because you're usually too busy blaming yourself."

"Hey, your fear of failure and my martyr guilt together? We might just be onto something."

She laughed, then sniffled. "I feel like an idiot. I just thought I could get through to her, and I wanted… I just wish you had answers. I wish I didn't fall apart when I don't get it exactly right."

"Don't we all? If you're going around thinking you're the only one who struggles and tries to hide it, or the only one who *should* hide it, you're wrong."

She looked at him, her eyebrows drawn together in a line creasing her forehead. Like she'd never heard such a thing in her whole life.

Maybe she hadn't. "I get it. Parenting your siblings is hard and messed up. It leaves you with stuff that feels untenable, but you just get through it."

"This is about you. Not me. You shouldn't feel the need to like…comfort me, because it isn't about me or what I'm dealing with."

He tilted his head and studied her. Was anything ever about her? He almost asked her, but figured she'd only put on that queen-of-the-manor look and waltz down to dinner. So he took a different approach. "I wish it was that simple. But it's about both of us. Because we're both here. So some days you get to fall apart, and some days it'll be my turn."

Her mouth trembled, then firmed. "What happens when we're both falling apart?"

"I figure we'll survive. What did you say to me earlier? Having a family, caring about each other, it means the balls don't shatter. Hell if that doesn't sound weird, but I think you get my point."

She nodded, looking down at her hands. "I just wanted to make everything okay."

"You can't. No one can. My mother was murdered. Your parents disappeared. Sometimes bad stuff just happens, and it'll never be okay." He lifted her hand to his mouth, kissed the bandage gently.

"No one's ever comforted me before, Mary. Not like you did earlier today. No one's ever taken care of me like you do. Zeke, Carlyle and I, we've always tried to take care of each other, but it's survival when you're moving around. When you're dealing with losing your parents. Even if we never find answers, I'll always be grateful that you've been a part of this these past few weeks, taking care."

Mary sniffled again. "She does know something, Walker. Carlyle. She got so angry. You don't get that angry if you don't know something. But I don't know how to get through to her. She's scared."

Walker nodded, feeling so many different things.

"She said she contacted HSS originally to protect you."

Walker frowned. "Protect me from what?"

"I don't know. But it wasn't about answers for her. It isn't about answers for her, I don't think. Which means…"

"She already has them."

"At least some of them."

"Well, we'll keep trying. See, you got something out of her after all."

Mary blew out a breath. Whatever she thought about that, she hid under that mask of coolness. "I think we should get down to dinner. They won't start without me and it's already late." She stood, but he couldn't quite let go of her hand so he was sitting on her bed and she was standing in front of him, looking down.

He knew he wanted to say something, but he couldn't find the right words. Something about how the past weeks had settled some restless part of him that had spent the last ten years—maybe longer—searching. He'd thought it was for answers, but now he wondered.

"You've lived without answers most of your life," he said softly.

She nodded solemnly.

He didn't have to ask her how. She had her siblings. She

loved them, cared for them and had them at the center point of her life. Family and love.

"It's different though," she said. She reached out and brushed her fingers over his temple with her free hand. "Whatever Carlyle is or isn't hiding, she's right about wanting to protect you. And the three of you aren't safe until whoever has been trying to hurt you is brought to justice."

He'd never thought of it like that. He'd thought of it like answers. Like protecting Carlyle. And Zeke. Never about justice. Because there was no justice in murder. Ever.

But Mary was right about one thing. This wasn't over until they figured out who'd been chasing him the past few years. Which made him think of what Mary had said a long time ago. That the people who'd shot at him at the apartment complex hadn't been very subtle. She'd questioned whether they'd really wanted him dead.

The relative quiet of the past few weeks made that theory hold even more weight. It also meant he was going to have to stop hiding out and start meeting some challenges head-on.

Once he figured out what the hell his sister was hiding.

Chapter Fourteen

Mary tried not to dwell on the mortification of Walker seeing one of her little breakdowns. They weren't common exactly, but they happened. Particularly when things were stressful. A little snowball of failures and she sometimes just needed to hide and cry it out.

He hadn't been horrified. She wasn't even sure he'd been surprised. He'd seemed to understand.

It was such a relief, such a wonder.

But she still hated that he'd seen her cry. Still hated that she'd failed him. And that she couldn't fix it. Because that moment existed—always, no matter what she did.

Strangely, that didn't make her want to hide from him. It was an embarrassment that didn't change how she felt around him. If anything it made her want to double down. Somehow be worthy of how easily he dealt with all her weaknesses—and she didn't know what to do with that, except go on as planned.

Walker spent the night in her room, in her bed, just like they'd planned. She woke up beside him the next morning, in the same room she'd been waking up in since she was a little girl, and she watched him sleep.

His dark hair was a wild, tangled mess against her pillowcase, his dark eyelashes fanned against his cheeks. The relaxed expression in sleep made him almost seem younger—

but then there were his broad, muscular shoulders, the sheer amount of space he took up without even being stretched out, that made it clear he was every inch a man.

A man who liked *her*. Trusted *her*. Even seeing the parts of her that she kept so ruthlessly hidden. And she understood now how her siblings had settled so quickly into a significant other, into intimacy and love.

She'd always thought romantic love was supposed to be hard or fraught or painful, but all it seemed to be was realizing someone loved you no matter what ugly parts of you they saw.

Not that Walker loved her, necessarily, but he certainly cared. And that was enough.

So, she was determined to talk to Carlyle again. To find some way to get through to the angry young woman. And if she didn't, at least she could tell Walker she'd tried. He seemed to think that was good enough.

She hoped she could convince herself it was good enough.

Eyes still closed, Walker shifted, unerringly moving to pull her closer to him. And even though she needed to get up, she let him. Because it was warm and safe here in this little cocoon before she let the real world invade.

He made a soft, contented noise, then pressed his mouth to her jaw, pulling her closer, holding her tighter. And it was far too tempting to turn in his arms, to press her mouth to his.

"I have to get up and make breakfast," she said against his mouth as his hands slid down her back.

"Sounds lame," he murmured.

"I like it."

"I know you do." He kissed her again but then he released her and yawned. "I should probably round up Carlyle and have a talk with her."

He swung out of bed, pulled on his clothes while Mary watched. He really was ridiculously handsome.

She got out of bed too. She had insisted on wearing pajamas last night. *Honestly, men.* She needed to run through the shower before she headed downstairs to make breakfast, but more than that she had to talk to him.

She crossed to him. "I'd like to try again with Carlyle. I mean, you can talk to her, too, but that might feel like ganging up. I just think I should take another shot at it."

He stopped zipping up his pants and looked at her with a searching gaze she couldn't quite figure.

"Yeah," he said. Then he pressed a hard kiss to her mouth, and she didn't know why that felt like soft, romantic confessions, only that it did. "You go ahead. We'll see how it goes and reevaluate."

Mary nodded. Then they just stood there, staring at each other.

"Mary…" he said.

And for some reason the way he said her name, the way he looked at her, made her heart jitter and she felt the need to hold her breath.

His eyebrows drew together and he looked from her eyes to the wall behind her as he sighed. "Zeke is going to want to do something. Probably something stupid. The kind of stupid I'd usually join him in."

She put her hand over his heart, because hers was tripping over itself as it had when Palmer and then Anna had gone off to the rodeo. Or when Grant had signed up for the military. Chasing that danger, that stupid risk. "I wish you wouldn't."

Walker paused, then put his hand over hers. He lifted it off his chest, pulled her palm to his mouth and pressed a kiss to it. "I'll do my best."

It wasn't a promise exactly, but she supposed it was something. And she held on to that something as she ran through the shower, as she went down to the kitchen and started prepping breakfast about fifteen minutes later than usual.

Being late didn't bother her this morning. She didn't let it. She was going to talk to Carlyle. She was going to get to the bottom of Walker's father.

And if she didn't, she'd just keep trying. Walker would be by her side either way. It put her in a good enough mood as she moved through breakfast. When Carlyle didn't show, she worried a little, but kept going through her routine.

Just about the usual time she went to the stables to give Walker and Carlyle their lessons, she finally decided to go on a search for Carlyle. Had the woman run away? Was she just hiding out because she didn't want to deal with Mary? Or was it something else?

Mary found her sitting on the back porch, two of Cash's dogs on either side of her. She had an apple in one hand and a mug of coffee in the other. She must have sneaked into the kitchen when Mary had been helping Izzy with her hair before school.

She was wearing ratty shorts and an oversize T-shirt definitely not fit for riding. "Aren't you going to get dressed for our riding lesson?"

"I thought…" Carlyle sat there looking very young for someone who was only four years younger than her. "I just figured you wouldn't want to do that today."

"Why not?"

Carlyle's frown deepened. "Because I was a bitch to you?"

Mary waved that off. It hadn't even occurred to her. "You can be mad at me, Carlyle. You can even be mean to me. I may not look it, but I have a thick skin." With some things anyway. "But I promised to teach you how to ride a horse,

and I don't go back on my promises. No matter how someone else behaves."

Carlyle clearly had nothing to say to that, so Mary
pointed to the spot on the stair next to her. "Can I sit down?"

"Your house," Carlyle replied, scooting over a little to
give Mary room. Mary settled herself on the stair, looked
out at the Hudson Ranch. Home. Her life, her love. Things
were changing, but this didn't, and maybe that was why it
didn't scare her to open up to the change—open her life, her
heart up to Walker and his family.

Besides, they fit right in.

"I see you got Walker to stay in the big house last night,"
Carlyle said, and it wasn't bitter exactly, but it definitely
wasn't happy.

"Yes," Mary replied, and she tried to think about it from
Carlyle's point of view. She tried to think of how she might
have felt if Jack had brought some woman home.

It was unfathomable, and she realized in this moment it
probably shouldn't be. "I can't even imagine if Jack brought
some woman home. I'm sure he dates. Or whatever it is men
do on their own time that I'd rather not think about when
it comes to my brothers. But he's never in all these years
brought anyone home or introduced us to anyone. I never
really thought about that, how lonely it must be for him."

"Oh, I'm not under any impression that Walker's been
alone," Carlyle replied loftily.

Mary tried not to frown at that, but it was hard. Carlyle
said it to upset her, and so she shouldn't let it land. But she
couldn't help hating the idea of Walker with other women,
even if he'd had every right to be. "No, I'm sure he hasn't
been alone. But being lonely and being alone are two different things."

Carlyle's shoulders slumped at that, and Mary couldn't
help but think she'd scored a point.

"I care very much about Walker. And how you feel about it doesn't really change anything more than you being rude does. But I understand the impulse and the discomfort, so I don't hold it against you."

They sat in silence for a while, and Mary let it stretch out. She petted Copper, watched some birds fly across the bright blue sky. And she waited, because if Carlyle wasn't trying to get under her skin or leaving, maybe she'd end up saying something worthwhile.

"Mary." Carlyle said her name very gravely, and when Mary looked over Carlyle was staring straight ahead. She had a mulish set to her chin, and her expression was determined. "If you really care about him, then you should be on my side on this."

"You haven't told me your side."

Carlyle nodded at that. "And I won't. Just know that it protects Walker." Finally, she turned so her gray-blue gaze met Mary's. She didn't share her brothers' dark eyes, or thick wavy hair. Of course, Anna favored their mother, while Mary and her brothers all looked more like their father. Such differences certainly happened.

"If we get any closer, everyone is going to get hurt," Carlyle said, very carefully. "If you give me some time, I can make sure that doesn't happen. The HSS was only supposed to buy me some time, but you're getting too close. Leave Don Daniels out of it. Go in another direction. Just for a little bit."

Mary absorbed that information that somehow told her so much and so very little. "If I give you time, if you make sure it doesn't happen, does that mean you're putting yourself in danger?"

Carlyle's expression went blank, but not blank enough for Mary not to read the answer in it.

She reached out, put her hand on the young woman's arm. "I know you want to protect your brothers—"

"You don't understand. You can't. Please, Mary. Let me handle this. I promise I know what I'm doing. They won't believe me because they think I'm perpetually twelve, but I know what the hell I'm doing, and I have to do it. But I can't if you and your family mess it up."

"I can't lie to Walker, Carlyle."

"Even to save him?" Carlyle demanded.

And that was quite the conundrum.

WALKER WAS ABOUT to get worried that he was first to the stables, considering he was always last. And Mary was never late for anything. He was already wound tight. He didn't know where Zeke was, and while that was normal, Zeke usually texted him back. He hadn't yet.

Walker checked his phone again for good measure.

Nothing.

He tried to busy himself by getting all three horses ready for the ride, but with every ticking moment, he felt closer and closer to panic.

Just about the time he was about to say *screw it* and call Mary, he saw her walking across the way, along with Carlyle, and the tight knot of anxiety in his chest eased. At least a little.

He hoped Mary had gotten through to Carlyle. Hoped there were answers to be found and quick. But more, he hoped, wished, prayed that this would be his real life. More than he wanted answers, he wanted Mary and his family to be in one place. Here. Together. Living whatever life had to throw at them.

Unfortunately, no matter how much he wanted that, he needed his baby sister safe. First and foremost. If she was holding back, if she knew something…

"Sorry we're late," Mary said by way of greeting. Her smile was genuine, but something like worry danced in her dark eyes.

Carlyle had gone straight for her horse, so Walker stayed by Mary and lowered his voice. "So, how'd it go? She tell you anything?"

Mary smiled at him, put her hand on his cheek. "A little. Nothing specific, but it was a good step. We'll get there."

Walker wasn't sure what to do with that nonanswer, but it was better than her crying, he supposed.

Then she surprised him and lifted to her toes and pressed her lips to his. The move surprised him because he didn't think she particularly liked being affectionate in front of people, and Carlyle might be distracted by horses, but she *was* right there.

"All right, lovebirds," Car said, mounting her horse in that easy way she had that made Walker feel guilty he hadn't been able to give her a childhood in some place like this. "Let's get this show on the road."

Mary nodded and kept smiling and moved to get on her own horse. She gave him a last few reminders as he mounted his. It was getting easier. More natural. He didn't know if he liked the rides so much for the sake of them or because Mary and Car were right here.

He supposed it didn't matter why. He just enjoyed this strange new part of his life.

They did their normal ride, Mary sometimes offering little lectures about what to do if different things happened while riding. She answered Carlyle's question about the cattle operation. For an hour, Walker put Zeke out of his mind and just relaxed.

But when they returned to the stables, Zeke was standing there, arms crossed over his chest. Clearly waiting for them. Clearly restless—which meant he'd found something and was ready to act.

Walker wanted to turn the horse around and canter in the opposite direction, but that was a luxury he didn't have. He pulled his horse to a stop and swung off. "What is it?"

Zeke jerked his chin at Mary and Carlyle. "Everyone should hear."

So Walker waited impatiently while Carlyle and Mary dismounted and walked over to Zeke.

"This morning I met with one of my contacts who's been digging into our father for me."

"You're involving other people?" Carlyle demanded.

Zeke shrugged. "If I have specific questions or concerns, some of my former North Star friends look into certain things for me. They're not really involved, but under the radar and necessary."

Carlyle clearly didn't like this, but she didn't say anything else and Zeke didn't look at her. He looked at Walker when he delivered the news. "Don's dead. Confirmed."

Shock rocked through him, but that was only part of the story. Walker could tell just by the way Zeke held himself. "When?"

This time Zeke's gaze turned to Mary. "Yesterday. Shot to death in his apartment. The cops think it was drug related, but I think otherwise."

Chapter Fifteen

"You think it's connected to what we found in his bank account?" Mary asked, trying to work through this new information and what it meant for moving forward.

It was possible Don was still their mother's murderer even if he was dead. But if he had died yesterday, it likely meant it was connected to what they were digging into

"I think it's connected to you looking. Not sure it's about what was found or not," Zeke returned. "And I think whoever is doing your computer work needs to stop."

"Palmer was very careful."

"Not careful enough," Zeke replied, clearly angry about it.

Mary could hardly blame him. "Let's all go to the big house. We'll sort this through with Palmer and see what—"

"Walker. Carlyle. We need to have a discussion." Zeke said it firmly, and in fact started walking away from the stables and toward the ranch hand cabin before they'd even responded.

"No," Walker returned just as firmly.

Zeke stopped and took his time turning to face Walker. Mary swallowed. She'd seen brotherly arguments that got out of hand before and could see this one brewing a mile away.

"We hired the Hudsons for a reason. We knew the risks,

and we also know how often it's no one's fault when things go sideways. We'll all head back to the big house and sort this through."

"You can go play house with your girlfriend, that's fine. But I won't be a part of it. I'm going to finally get to the bottom of this since apparently you can't."

"And neither could your little group of spies, could they?" Walker retorted.

"Let's just go up to the house and talk to everyone," Carlyle said. Mary thought she was maybe trying to sound bored, but she didn't.

"So now you're on his side?" Zeke demanded.

"No, I'm on *my* side," Carlyle returned, anger poking through. "While you both have your little fringe groups to run off to."

They faced off, three angry, hurting people who Mary knew deserved to have their fight. She had no place wading in and trying to diffuse things.

But she could hardly just stand there. So she moved into the center of them, being careful not to align herself with any single Daniels, and spoke to them all. Calmly.

"Guys. You just found out your father died. I know you all had a complicated relationship with him. I know this throws our current investigation into more flux than it has been. Tempers are high. Rightfully so. But you're all three going to regret turning on each other. And if you keep going, you'll regret what you end up saying."

Even Zeke had nothing to say to that.

Before Mary could say anything else, Walker spoke up. "I'm not turning on you, Zeke. I'm thinking about answers. For all of us. So, I'm going to go with Mary and discuss Palmer's computer work with him. Get HSS' take. You can go get North Star's theories, take some time to cool off or come with." He turned to Carlyle. "Same goes, Car. But

I know you know I'm always your side, no matter what. There's no fringe group. There's just the people who care."

Carlyle's gaze went from her brother to Mary. And Mary knew the woman didn't understand it yet, but Mary did care. Not just about Walker, not just because of Walker. Because she knew what it was like to be an orphan. To be raised by your older brothers. To try to make sense of a world that never really did care.

"I'll handle the horses. Meet you up there," Carlyle said with a little nod.

Zeke made a sound of disgust and continued to stalk away.

Walker took her arm gently. "Come on, Mary." She let him lead her toward the main house, but that didn't mean she was 100 percent comfortable with the move.

"Walker, you don't have to spare my feelings on this. Your brother—"

"Is angry and isn't thinking straight." He looked down at her, and this was serious Walker. The man she'd first met. Clear in his path, certain he was right. "Cutting your family out doesn't make sense for a wide variety of reasons, but mostly, we have to know what Palmer uncovered, how and who might have been able to pick up on that. We can't do that if we march off to our corner. We need to work together, or there was no point bringing you guys in. What's done is done. All we can do is keep trying. Zeke and I rarely agree on what that looks like."

Mary sighed and nodded. Walker would know his brother better than she did, certainly. She texted Palmer and Anna and asked them to meet her in the living room. She sent separate texts to Grant, Jack and Cash to keep them informed. They'd come if they had breaks in their schedules, and she would catch them up if they had to miss it.

"Walker…"

"I can't care that he's dead, Mary."

"I wouldn't expect you to. But caring and grieving aren't the only two responses to a death."

He took her hand, gave it a squeeze. "Maybe. I just… If he's dead, and it's because of this, we have to move. We have to act. Because eventually…"

Eventually whoever had killed Don Daniels would come after the rest of the Daniels clan. Mary wasn't sure she believed that, but she understood why he was reaching that conclusion.

"I know Zeke is blaming Palmer, and he has his doubts about us, but—"

"I don't," Walker returned. "Seriously. I've seen how you guys work. You're meticulous. If something slipped through, it's just the way it goes sometimes. Zeke has kept everything to himself, including working with his North Star group. So, he doesn't know, and that's on him."

"Are you always so good at taking things philosophically?"

Walker laughed, though there was no mirth in it. "I suppose I wasn't for a long while. But life has taught me it doesn't make much sense to be mad all the time. As far as I can tell, that's only ever hurt me. God knows whoever killed my mother doesn't care if I'm mad. So, I could blame Palmer. Or my brother. Or a million things, but at the end of the day, blame doesn't do much."

"Then let's work on finding justice."

"Yeah, let's do that."

THEY GATHERED IN the living room. As they waited for Carlyle, Mary made snacks. It was all very organized and somber. No one panicked. No one got defensive. The Hudsons, HSS, worked like a well-oiled machine.

Walker understood in these moments that Zeke had kept

himself purposefully away from this, because it was a stark reminder of all the ways they'd failed Carlyle. The ways they hadn't been able to give her something stable like this.

A few years ago, Walker might have had the same trouble. But something had changed when Carlyle had demanded she go out on her own. Walker had been forced to let go, and in that letting go he'd realized a person could only do what he thought was best any given moment.

Sometimes it was the right thing. Sometimes it wasn't. But you had to live with both.

Carlyle finally came in, and Walker couldn't read the odd expression on her face, but Mary called their little meeting to order and Walker had to focus on the task at hand.

"Don Daniels is confirmed dead. Happened yesterday and was clearly a murder. According to Zeke the police are thinking it's drug related."

"That'd be quite the coincidence," Palmer said darkly.

"Yes," Mary agreed, and it struck Walker as so silly she thought she couldn't do this. She was so good at keeping people on task, leading things to a conclusion.

"But something needs to be done," Mary continued. "Because either Don just happened to walk into something dangerous or us finding that payment started this domino of events."

"Digging into who paid him more like," Palmer said from where he stood by the front window, looking out.

"You think someone knew you were looking into them?" Walker demanded of Palmer.

"Me personally? No. That *someone* might be?" Palmer shrugged. "I can hide it well, but someone with more computer skills than me might have suspected someone gaining access. And I'm not finding anything, so whoever paid Don is good at hiding things."

"I don't know how Don could have gotten mixed up with

anything that fancy," Walker muttered irritably. "He was a deadbeat, abusive alcoholic with all of the sense of a rock."

"Well, if someone knocked him off because of this, likely Don was a pawn, not a player. Still, we'll want whatever police reports we can get our hands on. Carefully. I'll see what I can do." Palmer looked at Mary, and when she nodded, Walker realized Palmer had been asking Mary's permission to leave.

Once given, Mary turned to face Anna and her husband, Hawk.

"You had people after you," Anna said to Walker from where she was sitting on the couch. "A group would likely mean they were either pawns themselves or paid muscle. So, we're not looking for who's been after you. We're looking for who's paying *them*."

"So, likely that's going to be the same person that paid Don off," Walker said, frustrated because poking into that carefully meant taking time he wasn't sure they had anymore. Or worse, Zeke would start poking recklessly just to get the job done. "I need to go talk to Zeke. He's got some connections that he uses, but we need to make sure they weren't the reason Don got figured out either. We need to ensure everyone is safe. The rest is secondary."

Once upon a time he'd wanted justice for his mother, and it wasn't that he didn't still want that. It was just that justice didn't change anything. But if anyone got hurt in this, Mary's family or his own, that was a chance he couldn't bear.

"Walker."

He looked back at his sister, barely recognizing it was her that spoke when her voice was thready and uncertain. She looked pale, and he wasn't sure he'd ever seen quite so much upset in her eyes, at least not since she'd been a little girl. He crossed to her. "What is it, Car?"

"There's something…" She trailed off, looked over his shoulder at Mary. Walker glanced over his shoulder too. Mary had a kind of pleading look on her face, like she knew what Carlyle was going to tell him.

Like they had a secret.

"Don Daniels isn't my father," she said in a rush when he looked back down at her. "Mom told me before she died."

"What?"

"The guy who is?" She inhaled shakily. "He's… I'm willing to bet he's the guy paying people to follow you. And that he killed Don or had him killed. And if he thinks people are trying to find him, he'll want me next."

Chapter Sixteen

Mary didn't gasp, though she wanted to. She'd known Carlyle had a secret, and she'd hoped, in time, Carlyle would let her—and Walker—in on it. Before she'd gotten herself hurt or worse.

But this...

"Carlyle, what the hell?" Walker asked through gritted teeth.

"Mom told me that Don wasn't my dad. Right before she died, because she was afraid. And she said I had to keep it a secret."

Mary watched the hurt and worry and betrayal chase over Walker's face. She wanted to go to him, but she understood this was a brother-and-sister moment.

"Did *your* father kill our mother?" Walker asked in a rough voice.

"I don't know for sure. I know she was scared of him. And the timing... I don't know, Walker. I only know she told me I couldn't tell a soul. She said he'd kill all of us, so I always figured...yeah, it was him."

Walker's jaw set and Mary felt her own heart twist. What a terrible burden to put on a little girl, even if it was true.

Carlyle looked beyond Walker. "And he won't like that anyone is getting close. If he was behind those payments to Don..." Her gaze returned to Walker's, imploring. "He might not have evidence, but he'll know it's us. The fact that you two have been going in the wrong direction all this time is the only reason you're alive, I think, but if he has reason to think you know now… You have to stop Zeke." She grabbed Walker's hands. "It was one thing when he was busy with North Star, but now that that's done, he's going to get himself—maybe all of us—killed because he's going to find the answer."

Before Walker could react to that, Mary interjected. Because they still didn't have the full story. "Why is the secret so important to him?"

Carlyle's expression flickered, as she clearly was deciding how many details she wanted to divulge. But this was it. The breaking point. And Mary knew the only reason Carlyle was giving in was because she thought Zeke would get close enough for it to be dangerous.

"We need all the facts, Carlyle," Mary urged. "That's the only way to protect everyone."

Carlyle nodded, but her eyes were on her brother. "His name is… Connor Dennison."

"The *senator*?" Walker said in disbelief. "The grandson of Desmond Dennison? The husband of *Donna Kay*?"

Carlyle looked over at him and nodded. "Yeah, and that's the problem. He's richer than God. Has all the connections in the world between his and his father's politics and his wife's Hollywood status. He's basically a celebrity. And if I ever tell anyone he's my father, I'm not just dead, but anyone who might know is too." She looked up imploringly at Walker. "That's why I didn't tell," she said, her voice a pained whisper. "I couldn't tell."

"I don't understand. I was nowhere near the truth. Why would he try to stop me?" Walker asked, his voice still rough.

Carlyle hesitated. She chewed on her bottom lip, clearly

deciding what to keep a secret. But they could not deal in secrets any longer. Mary didn't want to butt into a family moment, but this was bigger now.

She took Carlyle's hand and led her over to the empty couch. She nudged the woman into a seat and then sat right next to her.

"Carlyle, I understand why you kept that secret and for so long. You wanted to protect your brothers. Of course you did. And you were young and impressionable. Maybe you made some mistakes, but we all do. It's not your fault that the adults in your life put you in a position where those mistakes might be fatal."

Her gray-blue eyes were filling with tears, though Carlyle was clearly fighting them. "But—"

"*But* nothing. It wasn't fair and it wasn't right, but now here we are. We need all the facts. We need them. It's the only way we can keep you and your brothers safe. I know you don't worry about protecting yourself—one of those Daniels family traits—but this isn't just about you anymore. And it hasn't been for a very long time. So, let's start at the beginning." She gave Carlyle's hand a pat. "When did your mother tell you?"

With her free hand, she waved Walker over. He moved like a hundred-year-old man, like he might fall to pieces at any moment, but when he sat down next to Carlyle, he took her other hand.

Because Carlyle needed support. She needed to believe this was the right thing.

And they all needed to hear it.

"It was right before she died. She was wanting to move again, and I…" Carlyle took a minute, Mary assumed fighting more tears. "I threw a fit. I had friends. I liked my teacher. I didn't want to move. And I wouldn't let up. You know how I was," she said to Walker.

He nodded with a rueful kind of smile.

"Mom lost it. Asked if I'd rather have friends or be dead."

Mary closed her eyes. What an awful thing to say to a little girl.

"She started talking about my father—she didn't give me a name, but I knew it wasn't Don. I knew...this was a secret, but she was so messed up over having to move again, so stressed about whoever she was running from, she just let it all out. She said he didn't know about me, but he'd follow her to the ends of the earth. That she'd never be free. He wanted her to pay for leaving him."

Walker muttered something foul under his breath, but Mary just gave Carlyle's hand a squeeze. "So, it's possible he killed her and didn't know you were his daughter?"

"More than possible, I think. If I'd... If I'd let it go, I don't think he'd have known. Or cared, maybe. But I just... When I turned eighteen, I..." She looked at Walker now. "Mom didn't tell me his name, just talked about him in a way that gave me some information to go on. I was just so mad about everything. Zeke doing that stupid North Star stuff. You struggling to make ends meet for *me*. Trying to convince me to go to college and stuff. So, I did some digging. Into where I was born and the like. Then I figured, why not ask the man she was married to when it happened."

"You went to Don?"

Carlyle shrugged jerkily. "He was in jail at the time, so it felt safe. He knew I wasn't his daughter, that much was clear. And he was more than happy to give up a name. I didn't believe him at first, because how would my dad be Connor Dennison? Even *I* knew who Connor Dennison was. But I dug into it, and it seemed as possible as anything, so I figured..."

She sucked in a breath, and the tears began to fall.

"I thought I could get some money out of him, you know.

I didn't… I just thought I was so smart." She quickly used the heel of her palm to wipe away the tears, clearly embarrassed by them.

Mary set a box of tissues in her lap.

"He denied it, threatened me, then had me followed on the way home. Luckily I was smarter than his thugs, but…"

"That's why you ran away that time. Not because you were mad about college. But because—"

"I knew if we stayed, he'd find you, find me. I think he's been trying to the past few years. But he needs me dead first, so I can't blow up his life. And he needs my death not to connect to yours or people will start digging, and come up with Mom. It's complicated, I think. That's why it's been so difficult. Last year… The threats to you kept getting closer, so I went to HSS with one of your aliases. I thought they'd find you and if you were dealing with them, I'd have time to figure out a way to take him down."

Mary's head was spinning. If she'd known Carlyle had been hiding all this… Well, she supposed it wouldn't matter. Carlyle wasn't going to tell anyone until she was ready.

Now they had to deal with the truth.

"I'm sorry," Carlyle continued, really crying now. "He doesn't care about you guys. He cares about making sure the truth doesn't get out—and I think that means he's the one who killed Mom. Because I'm just a secret kid, but she's an unsolved murder. Which means he's dangerous. He has to be careful because if anything connects to him his life is over. But he will kill us all if he thinks you know, if he can figure out how to get away with it, Walker, I have no doubt."

WALKER FELT LIKE he'd been gut punched. Maybe run over by a car. Never in a million years could he have anticipated all this.

Carlyle's hand was still in his, but he barely felt it. Barely felt anything. He glanced at Mary. Had Carlyle confided in her?

No, she seemed as shocked as he did. As everyone did. Because Anna and Hawk clearly were struggling to come to terms with Senator Connor Dennison being involved in this mess. And Zeke...didn't know.

Walker pulled Carlyle into a hug. Because she was crying. Because no matter how complicated this was, no matter how angry he was at her, Mary had been right. It had been wrong that their mother had put that kind of burden on a little girl.

"We'll sort through this mess. It'll be okay."

"I can't lose you and Zeke too," she said into his chest. "Please. I know how good you guys are at this stuff, but he will win. The only reason we've been able to avoid him this past year is because we've been split up, because of Zeke's North Star connections, and how far off you've been from the truth. But if he was behind that money, he thinks you know. Him being careful won't last with the truth out. Men like him always win."

Walker wished he could argue with her. But money and power had more sway than just about anything in this world, and he might have a lot of skills, but he didn't have either of those two things to go along with it.

He broke the embrace and looked into her eyes intently. "I have to stop Zeke before he does something without the full picture. I'll be back, but I need you to promise me to stay put."

"Walker—"

"I'm serious. You stay put. Promise?"

She stared at him, eyebrows drawn together, some new emotion joining all the fear and misery in her eyes. "Fine," she muttered.

Walker nodded, got up and strode to the door. He was

already off the porch and a ways across the yard when he heard Mary call his name.

He stopped and turned to see her standing there on the porch, wringing her hands. "I didn't know," Mary said. "She didn't tell me fully."

Walker nodded. It did make him feel better, though maybe it shouldn't. Still, he stayed where he was with enough distance between them he couldn't get a full read on her expression.

He couldn't focus on Mary. He had to get to Zeke. He had to focus on *this*, not her.

"Do you want me to come with you? I could—"

Walker shook his head. "You're a hell of a peacemaker, Mary, but I think maybe peace isn't what we need right now."

"You shouldn't fight with your brother."

She was clearly worried about that. About him. But she didn't understand. Couldn't. And he didn't know how to explain any of this. "We'll see."

He heard her sigh, but he didn't let that change his course of action. He walked back to the cabin, hoping he wasn't too late. Hoping he had the words to get through to his brother.

Because just like he'd known Carlyle was hiding things, even if he hadn't known *what*, he knew Zeke had more information than he'd let Walker in on. But not as much as Carlyle.

Walker had always thought his siblings kept him in the loop when they weren't together. Even while he'd not been keeping them in the loop of what he'd been up to.

He really should have known better, but he supposed that's why they'd all gone their separate ways last year. To keep their secrets. To protect one another. At least they'd sort of succeeded considering they were all still breathing.

But Carlyle was right. That couldn't last forever. Not

when a man had the kind of power and money Connor Dennison did.

So the time for secrets was officially over.

Walker entered the cabin to find Zeke loading his gun, an array of items on the table as he was clearly packing a bag to leave.

"You should have come, Zeke. Carlyle dropped a hell of a bomb."

"Is it about Senator Dennison?"

Walker stared at his brother for a good minute before he could make his mouth work. "How…"

"I just got the name from my North Star contacts. It was hidden well, but that's the origin of Don's payment, so he's connected somehow. So, no, I didn't need to stay."

"You do because that's only half the picture."

Zeke kept loading guns, clearly not impressed.

"Carlyle says Connor Dennison is her biological father."

Zeke's hands stilled and he raised his gaze to Walker. "What?"

"Mom told her before she died, that it wasn't Don. Apparently Dennison didn't know, but then Carlyle…" Walker didn't want to tell Zeke, because he didn't want him to be too hard on Car, but secrets weren't helping them. They needed to work with all the information. Together.

Well, him and Zeke. Carlyle would stay behind and Mary and her family would protect her. And somehow… Somehow he and his brother would make this right.

So he relayed everything Carlyle had said up at the main house. Zeke's expression betrayed nothing, except a cold kind of fury.

"We've got to do something, Walker. We can't hide anymore. *I* can't hide anymore. He could have killed you, but he didn't. I think he could have had me, too, but he didn't.

We can chalk that up to our own skills, or we can look at the more reasonable answer."

"It was too risky for him because we didn't know. But he knows Carlyle knows enough. He knows someone has been poking into those payments. He wants her gone, and us, too, if he can swing it."

"And he won't rest until he gets his way. Some rich powerful guy who hasn't made a move yet? He's being careful nothing comes back to him. We have to make it come back to him. It won't be easy. It might not even be possible. But I've got to try." Zeke went back to his guns.

"When are you leaving?" Walker asked, resigned. Because sometimes there wasn't a good approach to something. Sometimes, you just had to make the wrong decision with someone, *for* someone.

"The minute it's dark."

"I'm coming with."

Zeke paused in his packing. He studied Walker carefully. "You sure about that?"

Walker thought about Carlyle. About how everything had changed after that fire on her eighteenth birthday. About the fact that she'd known all this time what that something was. She'd kept it to herself thinking she'd somehow protect him and Zeke.

And he had no doubt, because she was a Daniels even if she wasn't Don's daughter, that she'd been content enough in the knowledge that if someone died, it would be her. Not her brothers.

He'd come to the same conclusion about himself the closer someone had been on his tail over the past year. So no doubt Zeke had the same thoughts when he'd been out there doing North Star things and who knew what all else.

Which was why Zeke couldn't go it alone. Neither of them could, much as Walker didn't want to go. Didn't want to throw himself into danger anymore. Because he'd found Mary, found a life here.

But none of that mattered if they didn't find a way to protect Carlyle. None of that mattered if he let Zeke go at it alone. He could hardly let his family's issues put the Hudsons in danger for the foreseeable future either. "I'm sure. I've got to get some stuff from the main house, and I'm going to get a few more details about this guy from Palmer. Don't leave without me, got it?"

"She going to talk you out of it?" Zeke asked skeptically.

"No." Mary might try, but Walker had made up his mind.

Chapter Seventeen

When Walker returned, Mary was making dinner. She could tell from his expression she wasn't going to like whatever he had to say.

"Where's Car?"

"I tried to convince her to lie down for a bit, but that didn't work, so Cash offered her some work over with the dogs."

Walker nodded. "That's probably best. Keep her mind busy anyway."

Mary studied him. She could see a little too much good-bye in his eyes and she desperately wanted to find a way to change it. So she crossed to him, put her hands on his chest. "I told this to Carlyle, but I hope all three of you know it. You have a place here. A life."

He put his hands over hers, and she saw the regret, but also that his decision was already made. "Zeke is going after Dennison, with or without me. I can't…"

Mary had to work very hard to hold on to her composure, because she couldn't argue with this, much as she wanted to. "You can't let him go alone."

His eyes were soft, his words genuine as he curled his fingers around hers. "I'm sorry."

"I know." She had to swallow at the lump clogging her throat. "And I understand. He's your brother. You have to protect him, and I know he'll protect you right back. It's something you both need to do." She hated it, didn't want him to do it, but understood. She'd hardly let any of her siblings go off into something so dangerous without trying to alter the course. Granted, she'd use her *words* to not go along with them, but maybe there were no words to stop Zeke. "Will you tell Carlyle?"

"No. She's in the most danger. I need her to stay here. I need you and your family to protect her at all costs. Dennison might be happy to take us out given the right circumstances, but Carlyle is who he really wants."

Mary didn't want to scold, didn't want to tell him he was wrong. Not in this moment where her heart felt bruised, and she knew his did too. But… "You leaving her out of the equation isn't going to go over well."

"We aren't leaving her out. She's the target, so she has to be protected. I know she won't see it that way, but that's the way it is."

"Did it occur to you she might want to protect herself?"

Walker's expression changed. *Detached* was the only word Mary could think of to describe it. Because she'd seen it on Jack's face too.

"I'm sorry," Mary said. "I don't want to argue with you. But I think you should tell her."

"So *she* can argue with me?"

"Walker."

"I don't have time, Mary. If I'm not back soon, Zeke will just assume you talked me out of it and he'll leave. I can't let that happen."

Mary swallowed. The truly frustrating thing was that she understood *all* their points of view. And none of them were totally wrong.

"I just had to say something before I go."

Mary took a step back, because she knew this was some

stupid goodbye, and she refused to say it. Still, she couldn't back fully away because his grip on her hands tightened.

She shook her head. "Don't say goodbye because you'll be right back. And you'll keep in touch. And you'll let us help you. I won't accept anything else. So, there's nothing to say."

He heaved out a sigh, and she knew it was not one of acceptance, so she tried to tug her hands away, but he held firm.

"Mary, I love you."

Her mouth dropped open as shock wound through her. She definitely wasn't trying to pull away any longer. *Love.* He'd said... "Walker—"

"I don't want you to say anything to that," he said firmly. "Whether you feel it or not. I know how you'd smooth anything over, and I don't want that right now. I just want you to say it in a moment you really mean it—if you mean it, okay? When it just sweeps through you, and you can't think of a single other thing to say. Not now. You pick *your* moment. This was mine."

"Walker..." How could she not mean it? But that lump in her throat had grown exponentially, and he was shaking his head.

"You gotta give me that, Mary."

She didn't know how, in this moment, not to give him everything he asked for. So she could only let him pull her into him, lift her mouth to his in what felt way too much like a goodbye, except... If she didn't say it, it meant he *had* to come back.

"I'll be back," he said against her mouth, as if he could read her thoughts. He pulled away, looked her in the eye. "Know that. Believe that. Okay?"

She nodded. She couldn't have spoken if she'd tried. Then he released her, quickly turning and exiting the kitchen.

He didn't hesitate. Didn't look back. And she thought she knew him well enough to understand he couldn't, or he'd be tempted to change his mind.

But he couldn't because he had to protect Zeke. Who wanted to protect Carlyle, who wanted to protect both her brothers. A never-ending circle that would only end in sacrifice.

When it wasn't right. None of them should have to sacrifice.

Mary turned off all the burners, leaving dinner half-prepared. She texted Dahlia asking her to finish everything up when she got the chance. She found Anna and Hawk, gave them some instructions on how to run the place without her.

Because like hell were Walker and Zeke doing this on their own. It hadn't gotten them anywhere all this time, so now…

They'd hired HSS. They were going to get the full Hudson treatment. Which meant no one did anything on their own.

Once she had all the plans made, she went in search of Carlyle. Since she wasn't with Cash and Izzy or any of the animals, Mary went up to the guest room and knocked on the closed door.

Carlyle opened it, but only a crack. "I think I'll skip dinner tonight," she said.

"I didn't come up here to tell you about dinner."

Carlyle frowned a little. "You didn't?"

"Your brothers are going to do something stupid."

Carlyle nodded, let the door open farther. Which was when Mary saw that she'd packed up what few belongings she'd brought here. "It's okay, I'm going to go after them. They want to protect me, but this is *my* fight. Maybe it shouldn't have to be, but my mother left it to me. So it's mine now."

"You're not going after them," Mary said firmly. "We both are."

IT HAD BEEN a while since Walker and Zeke had done anything together. In fact, come to think of it, they really hadn't
since Zeke had become an adult. Because he'd been gone
in the military, then he'd been out in the world doing North
Star stuff.

Walker couldn't think of his brother as a stranger, but
it was a strange moment in time to realize that Zeke had
turned into a full-grown man in all the time apart.

"So, do you have a plan?" Walker asked him.

"Mallory is getting me some intel on Dennison from a
computer expert she knows. Right now, I know Dennison
is in Colorado, so that's where we're headed."

Their cousin Mallory was the one who'd gotten Zeke
hooked up with North Star in the first place. One of the few
people their mother had kept in touch with over the course
of their many moves had been her sister—Mallory's mother.
Mallory had actually been the one to find Carlyle when she'd
run away at eighteen.

It still floored Walker that she'd run away because of
Connor Dennison. The fire had to have been Dennison.
Don being dead had to be him too. It was all…too much.

So, he focused on his brother, and his brother's 'connections.'

"I thought the whole North Star thing got disbanded,"
Walker said to his brother, trying to focus.

Zeke shrugged. "Did, but that doesn't erase our skills.
Everyone's all married and popping out babies, doing some
search and rescue, so they're not going to be running into
danger, but they can still get me intel when I need it. Or get
me in touch with the people who can."

"And when we have this intel, what do we do with it?"

Zeke's hands tightened on the wheel as he drove. But he
clearly didn't have an answer for that.

"We can't go in half-cocked. We'd end up dead, that only leaves Carlyle alone."

"Or maybe something they can pin on this guy."

Walker winced in the dark of the car. He understood that thought process. He would have had the same exact one if he didn't want to get back to the Hudson Ranch as much as he wanted to protect his sister.

He had something to live for now. He'd always wanted to protect Carlyle, but it had been in a selfish kind of way. The need to be the savior, the one who did it. The one who found the answers.

Now... He didn't care who found those answers, as long as they had them. He had learned to take off the blinders and see not just his own wants and needs, but Carlyle's.

Which, of course, led him to be haunted by Mary's voice telling him he should talk to Carlyle. Include her in this whole thing. He should have. He knew that.

But he wouldn't have been able to bear it, and neither would Zeke. Maybe he was a hypocrite—but sometimes life was hard, and you had to be one.

"I'm guessing if you asked Car she'd rather have us alive than have this guy in jail."

Zeke didn't say anything to that, though a muscle in his jaw twitched.

"What are you really running from?" Walker asked, even knowing Zeke wouldn't tell him. Even knowing that Zeke might not fully understand himself. Walker had gone through that, too, because sometimes you just had to run and it took something, or someone, to finally ask you why.

Zeke sent him a sideways glance, then looked back at the road. "I'm not running *from* anything. I'm running toward the truth. And ending this, once and for all. If he's behind our mother's murder, that's it."

Walker considered his brother's words. The word *end*

most of all, because even if they somehow thwarted a millionaire celebrity politician, it wasn't an end. They still had to pick up the pieces and live.

"So you're heading toward a new beginning, then," Walker surmised. "You know, beginnings can be scary when your future can be anything. Much easier when you see what you want it to be."

"I'm glad shacking up with a woman has clarified your future for you, Walk, but—"

"Call it shacking up. Call it whatever you want, but you know it's more than that. I don't need to sit here and have a heart-to-heart about it, but I love Mary. And if I can figure out what the hell to do with my life, and she'll have me, I plan on making that permanent."

"Jesus, you've known her a month," Zeke muttered.

Walker laughed, was surprised he could under the circumstances. "Who knows how long we've got, so why worry about how long something's been?"

"Awful fatalistic for a guy who's talking about futures."

"Someday you'll be old too."

Zeke snorted—the closest Walker figured he'd get to making his brother laugh, so he'd take it as a win.

They drove the rest of the while in silence. Walker hoped Zeke was considering some real plans, not just doubling down on his impulsive actions. Walker didn't think there was any hope of talking Zeke out of confronting Connor Dennison, but maybe they could do it in a way that didn't spell ruin.

Zeke pulled off the highway, drove down some winding dirt and gravel roads. When he finally pulled to a stop, it was in front of a quaint little cabin in the middle of nowhere, illuminated by both the moon and security lights.

"This is not what I was expecting." Walker had anticipated spending the night in a tent in the woods. A vacant motel in some ghost town. Not a decent-enough-looking house. He studied his brother. "We're not committing a crime, are we? Because I didn't sign on for a little light B&E."

"What can I say? I've got connections," Zeke said with a shrug as he got out of the car.

Walker had always known this, but it was strange seeing how helpful those connections were. A reminder they'd lived much different adulthoods.

Still, he followed his brother onto the porch. Zeke punched in a code on a hidden keypad, then once inside did the same on a visible one. "We'll spend the night here, sleep and eat, then make it to Colorado tomorrow."

"You got fancy digs there too?"

Zeke grinned. "Yeah, I do."

Walker shook his head, then moved into the kitchen. He was starving, as they'd skipped out on Hudson family dinner. He missed Mary's cooking already. Canned soup and slightly stale crackers were hardly a replacement. But he ate, while Zeke filled him in on the information Mallory had gotten on Senator Dennison.

"I'm not sure how we're going to get access to a guy who has personal bodyguards," Walker said. "What about involving the cops? You've got proof he's the guy behind the payment to Don. They can look into it."

"But then they might look into *how* I got information that isn't exactly legal for me to have. Something we could get around when we were North Star, but a little harder to fudge now that we're not. I could get around it eventually, but if Dennison knows we're looking, if he killed Don…"

Walker scowled into his soup. Likely Carlyle was next. "Maybe we shouldn't have left her behind."

Zeke shook his head. "We'll keep the man's attention

right here." He stilled, the spoon halfway to his mouth, eyes narrowing.

Walker didn't have to ask him why, he'd seen the flash of headlights against the window. "Get your gun."

Zeke was already moving for his bag while Walker crouched so there would be no shadow in the window.

Then a knock sounded on the door. A loud, brash, insistent knock.

"How the hell did Carlyle find us?" Zeke muttered irritably, striding for the door just behind Walker.

Walker jerked the door open, but then just stood there, mouth hanging open. Carlyle looked pissed, but he expected that. What he didn't expect was Mary to be standing behind her with that kind of smile that seemed to say, *I know more than you do, of course*.

"Looks like you're going to need a bigger boat," Carlyle announced, stepping inside and dropping her bag on the ground.

Chapter Eighteen

Even in the midst of danger and concern, Mary found some enjoyment at the utter shock on Walker's and Zeke's faces. If they were surprised, then at least she'd succeeded at something.

"How the hell did you find us?" Zeke demanded. Anger pumped off him, which Mary had anticipated, as had Carlyle. In fact, on the long drive, Carlyle had laughed over the idea of Zeke blowing a gasket.

Currently, he was holding it together, but barely. Mary didn't think the *hows* were going to make him feel any better.

"Well," Mary said, making sure to be extra calm in the face of Zeke's fury, "I may have had Cash put a tracker in Walker's car before you left."

Both Walker and Zeke stared at her like she'd grown a second head. Carlyle slung her arm over Mary's shoulders.

"She's got a secret sneaky side. I love it."

Mary knew neither Zeke nor Walker loved it. She could also tell they were already scrambling to figure out how to get rid of them, but Mary would not be gotten rid of. She'd made a plan, and she, Carlyle and her siblings were part of that plan. And she was sticking to it, no matter how angry Walker looked.

His expression was hard, and his dark eyes pierced hers as he glared at her. "I want to talk with you. Alone."

"Ooh, you're in trouble," Carlyle said in a singsongy whisper, clearly enjoying some part of all this friction.

Mary wished she could have Carlyle's reckless "don't care about people's opinions" attitude, but it wasn't in her. Even knowing she was right, her heart twisted at Walker's cold voice.

Walker glared at his sister, but he took Mary by the arm and led her outside. It was late, but the stars and moon shone along with some security porch lights that created a little cocoon of light outside.

Walker immediately let go of her arm, and the first little alarm bells went off that he was *really* angry. Not that she was surprised. She just had to brace herself for it.

"I can't believe you'd not just risk yourself, but Carlyle," he said. No, not said. That was too tame. She couldn't call it full-on yelling, but it was definitely an angry scold.

"I'm sorry," she said, and she was. Not for doing what she'd done, but that he couldn't see he was wrong. "But I told you I didn't think you should leave Carlyle behind or out of this. She was going to follow you one way or another. This way was much safer. Not only was I with her, but since Cash dropped the tracker, we knew exactly where you were."

"You should have stayed put. You should have made her stay put," he said, closer to a yell this time.

"How?"

His mouth firmed, because—she knew—he didn't have an answer for that. No one *made* Carlyle do anything.

"You said you understood."

"Understanding and agreeing are two different things, Walker. I also told you keeping Carlyle out of this was not the right choice. She was coming after you, one way or another. I think, deep down, you had to have known that."

"Don't use that schoolteacher voice on me. Don't lecture me. You shouldn't have followed us. You should have stayed put."

"So you two could handle it all yourselves?" she returned. Not with his anger and frustration, but with that schoolteacher voice he hated so much. "Because you're so much better and more important than everyone else?"

He inhaled through flared nostrils, and the anger pumped off him in waves, but Mary also understood while he might be angry at her, most of all he was just angry with the situation. So, she didn't take it personally.

She understood too well all the conflicting emotions of wanting to protect, of being protected.

"Are you done yelling at me?" she asked calmly, hands clasped in front of her.

He glared at her. "I haven't decided."

He stood there, arms crossed over his chest, a mix of anger and worry on his face. And that's when she felt it. Back at the ranch he'd told her to wait for a moment when she felt swept by love. And this was it. She was swamped by the need to protect him, save him, all so she could bring him home and get to the work of building a life with him.

She crossed to him. Placed her palms on his chest. "I love you, Walker."

"Mary, I said—"

"I know what you said. You said say it when you mean it. You said pick your moment. This is my moment. I can't let you do this alone. I can't let you just follow Zeke because you need to be there to watch him fling himself into danger. If we all work together—*all* of us—I think we can fix this. So, I'm here because I love you. I'm letting you vent at me because I love you. And I understand because I love you."

He hadn't moved, hadn't let his arms uncross, and still she felt him soften underneath her hand.

"That's not playing fair," he muttered.

"Then it's a good thing we aren't playing. This is serious and dangerous. And I have a plan. But you have to let us help you. *All* of us."

"Are your siblings going to come pouring out of the clown car?"

"Not yet, though we're working on something. But I want it to be a team effort. Which means Zeke has to be on board."

"Good luck. If I thought I could get him on board, we wouldn't be here." He finally dropped his arms, then he reached out and pulled her close. He framed her face with his big, calloused hands.

"I need you to understand, if you got hurt in this, I won't be able to live with myself. It's not about thinking we're better. It's about knowing what it is to lose." She saw that raw pain in his face and realized, maybe for the first time, the differences in their experiences. Yes, her parents had disappeared, and they were likely dead, but she didn't know. She didn't know how it had happened or if it was true. It was all question marks.

He knew. He'd had to deal with the aftermath of murder. Why wouldn't he be that much more protective of anyone mixed up in this mess? He knew that finality of death too intimately. There was no finality in all her life.

Still… The thought of him getting hurt or worse was too much to let her mind dwell on.

"You don't think I feel the same way?" She covered his hands with her own. "But I know you have to do whatever it takes to end this. So know that I have to be here." She sucked in a deep breath. "I know you won't like our plan, but it's better than two hardheaded men wading in without any sense of *why*."

"I've got a damn good sense of *why*."

"No, you have a good sense of who. Of what. But not why. We need to find that why, Walker. Which is why…" Oh, he was really going to hate this. Argue with her. Explode, maybe. But it was best they did this with the little slice of privacy they had now. Best to try to get him on her side without Zeke and Carlyle interfering.

"That's why I'm going to meet with Senator Dennison. As an ambassador for HSS who has some questions to ask him about an investigation we're handling."

WALKER STILL HAD his hands on Mary's face, but he was pretty sure he'd had some kind of stroke. "I must have heard you wrong, Mary."

She held his gaze with that calm, certain one of hers. "You didn't."

He dropped his hands, stepped away from her. She clasped her hands in front of her again, that schoolteacher look firmly in place.

He tried to mimic it so he could be the calm one. "I think the hell not." Okay, maybe not calm.

"I understand your knee-jerk reaction."

"It's far from knee-jerk. Mary, it is more than likely that this man killed my mother *and* father. He wants my sister dead. And the only thing stopping him is that he hasn't been able to figure out a way to get away with it yet. You think anyone is going to be okay with you walking into the lion's den like this?"

"Carlyle is okay with it. Anna is okay with it."

"You're missing a hell of a lot of names on that very short list."

"My brothers aren't opposed. They just want one of them to go with me. I didn't think that was the smartest idea. I think you should come with me."

Walker scrubbed his hands over his face. Maybe he was having that stroke. "Mary—"

"Hear me out. You're the client, right? Joe Beck. He likely knows that alias. If you come with me, and all our questions are about the money Don was paid—nothing about his murder or Carlyle's parentage—it's possible we convince him this is all we know, all we suspect. We act like we don't know he might know who you are, who your aliases are and so on. We make ourselves look out of the loop and barking up the wrong tree so he backs off."

Walker blew out a breath. His insides were tied tight at the thought of Mary putting herself in any kind of danger, but she was being so rational and so reasonable. She'd looked at him with that calm, earnest gaze and said *I love you.*

He wanted to believe it was manipulation, but it wasn't. It was just…whatever existed between them. They understood each other, they fit.

So he didn't let himself fly off the handle—like he might have with Carlyle. Like he had in the past. He tried to find some maturity. Some sense.

He tried to understand, tried to be on her side. He tried to get over the terrifying fear he was putting her in his mother's shoes.

But no matter how hard he worked to understand, he knew his brother wouldn't. "Zeke won't go for this."

"We have to try. Listen to me. Jack is looking into what can be done from a legal standpoint. Anna and Hawk are looking at the less legal avenues we can go down. Palmer is working on some surveillance or something that would allow us to get Connor Dennison saying something incriminating on video or audio. We're going down all these avenues, but we all have the same goal."

Walker didn't know what to say to that. For so long, his inclination had been to handle things on his own. He knew his siblings shared that MO of withdraw and figure it out yourself. It was their protective mechanism.

But maybe a limiting one, too, he realized now.

Could he get that through to Zeke? "Zeke has some connections of his own from when he worked with a secret group. Maybe we can have him, Anna and Hawk work with them to handle the less than strictly legal avenues. If he's occupied with that, maybe he won't totally fight me on this."

"Or I could go alone. He wouldn't have to know and—"

Walker shook his head. "You know that's a no-go. From me. From your family. From common sense."

"I think common sense says that if Dennison has been this careful for this long he's not going to off me the minute I meet with him."

"But he could, Mary. That's the thing. If he killed two people, he's capable. And capable of getting away with it."

"Then we have to get Zeke on board. Then we have to work as a team. So we can *all* be safe. Now and forever."

It sounded too good to be true, just as it had when she'd said she loved him. That was too good to be true, but it was real. He reached out, pulled her to him. She leaned her cheek against his chest, relaxed into him. Here in the middle of nowhere with the night and danger creeping around them.

So, he pressed his mouth to hers. Because she was here, and they were going to face this together. Complicated. Terrifying. But somehow… Right.

"Say it again."

"Say what again?" she returned, a little primly, clearly knowing exactly what he wanted.

He smiled against her mouth. "You know what."

Her lips curved and she met his gaze. "I love you, Walker."

That was a miracle, so why not believe they could make a few more happen? "I love you too."

Chapter Nineteen

Mary knew how to lead a meeting. She also knew how to deal with surly members of that meeting. She was terrified, but it was easy enough to keep that below the surface. Because the important thing wasn't if she was scared or not. It was what needed to be done.

"I'll try to set up the meeting as soon as possible," she told Walker's siblings as they sat in the cabin, listening to her plan, "but in my experience setting up meetings with people who don't want to meet, his people will try to put me off. There's also the issue of how many people I'll have to go through to get to Dennison himself. But Jack has had some conversations with the local police, and we can use some names there to put some pressure behind it."

"If I went, he'd see me," Carlyle said somewhat belligerently from her spot curled up on an armchair.

"Yes," Mary agreed. "And potentially do whatever it took to have you killed, then and there. Not to mention, turn his attention on everyone involved. If it's just Walker and me, we have the chance to convince him no one knows anything but you."

"That still leaves her a target," Zeke pointed out, all sharp edges and barely restrained anger. But he *was* restraining it, so that was something.

"That's why this is only step one, Zeke. Now, are your friends going to help or not?"

"I gave them Hawk's information. Anyone who wants to will get in touch with him. A lot of people, our cousin included, are pretty involved in their family life and can't really put boots on the ground. But they'll do what they can from the background."

"I think that's good. We don't want to raise suspicion with lots of people getting involved."

"Okay, let's say this sad little plan works," Zeke said, clearly dismissive not just to be a jerk, but because he was worried. "Dennison believes only Carlyle knows something. He hides his connection to Don or whatever. Then what?"

"While we're dealing with Dennison, HSS will continue the investigation, collect any evidence and data we can. If he's occupied with what we're questioning him about, he might not notice that. We get the police involved, carefully. See if we can get a search warrant for his house or office or anywhere he might have evidence. We put together a case against Dennison. One that can take him down, no matter what kind of fancy lawyers he hires. And while all that's going on, we try to get something incriminating on tape."

"And if none of that works?"

"Then we move on to plan B, Zeke," Walker said, or growled, before Mary could. "You know as well as I do there's no foolproof plan. There's only going forward."

"He'll want to meet on his turf, but not anywhere that might be incriminating," Mary continued, not bothered by the complaints or the growling. In her mind, it wouldn't be a meeting with siblings if people didn't argue.

"You can't meet anywhere that's his. Not his house or office," Carlyle said. "It's too dangerous. A guy with that much money can make people disappear in his own space. Especially if it's an appointment and he knows you're coming. I'm pretty sure the only way I escaped back then was because he didn't know I was coming and kind of broke in."

"It's HSS policy to meet in a neutral spot. So, we'll leave finding one to you and Zeke," Mary said. "Once we get to town, you'll scout out a few good spots we can suggest to meet him at."

"Based on the quiet of the past month, we can reasonably assume Dennison didn't know where you were, so following us would be tough. We'll get to town and lay low for a day first, just to make certain."

Mary didn't balk at Walker making those kinds of decisions. It was a solid plan, so she nodded.

"I've got a car switch planned for the morning," Zeke said, though Mary could tell it was with some reluctance he was handing over information. "It's possible he's got someone on the lookout for Walker's junker, or any of the cars in his little fleet."

"You have a fleet?" Mary asked, raising an eyebrow at him.

Walker grinned at her. "I have an array of a lot of things."

She couldn't help but smile back. But she didn't let it fully distract her. "All right, that's the plan then. Get some rest. What time do we need to leave?"

"Meeting my contact at a place about three hours away." Zeke checked his watch. "So, maybe a two-hour nap. Security is set so no one needs to stay up for watch duty. Car, you're going to have to take the couch as long as Mary and Walker are doubling up."

"How am I still getting stuck on the couch?"

"Because you're still the smallest," Walker replied, giving her a brotherly nudge.

He got to his feet and took Mary's hand.

"You know, everyone should *sleep*," Zeke said, staring at Walker pointedly.

Mary worked hard not to blush, but Walker said nothing as he led her away from the kitchen and toward a door. He opened it and pulled her inside the cozy little bedroom.

"I imagine you packed some kind of bag full of essentials," he said, and he waited for her to step inside before he closed the door behind her.

"I did, but I don't really need anything for a nap."

He nodded and didn't say anything else. He didn't even look at her really. He just settled onto the bed and motioned for her to do the same.

Mary didn't have the first clue how anyone would sleep— let alone for two short hours. It'd likely take her that long just to calm her brain down enough to close her eyes. Still, she crawled into bed next to him. He was lying on his back, staring at the ceiling. Likely he was thinking, but still…

"You're uncharacteristically quiet."

His mouth curved slightly, then he turned onto his side to face her. "I guess you throwing yourself headlong into danger will do that to a guy."

"You'll be with me."

He nodded, but there wasn't any levity in his expression. Just a grim kind of acceptance, she supposed. She reached out, touched her palm to his cheek, needing to find some kind of comfort for him. "We're going to do everything carefully, safely. You've made it this far, Walker. Now you have all this help. It's a positive."

He nodded, and she knew he didn't agree—or at least, couldn't find it in himself to have that kind of hope. She could hardly blame him.

His gaze met hers, dark and assessing. "You're not nervous about failing?"

"You told me there is no failure except giving up." She forced a smile. "I'm working very hard on believing that."

His mouth curved, a little glimmer of mischief in his

eyes popping up. *There* was Walker. He pulled her close and pressed his mouth to hers, his hands sliding under her shirt.

"I'm pretty sure Zeke told us no funny business," she said primly against his eager mouth.

Walker grinned. "I don't recall ever listening to my brother."

THEY SLEPT—WELL, some people did—then got on the road. Zeke drove since he wouldn't give them details on where they were making the car swap.

Walker tried to relax. Trust his brother, trust the Hudsons. Go with the flow. Not worry about bridges they hadn't crossed yet.

But Carlyle was quiet, her expression opaque.

She was damn well making him nervous.

After three hours, Zeke started making turns onto gravel and dirt roads. Mountains were in the distance, but all around was nothing more than fields.

But after a bit more driving, an old, dilapidated barn came into view. Zeke said nothing, just drove straight for it, and then onto the grass and into the wide opening on the side of the barn.

Inside there was a car, and a woman dressed all in black throwing darts at a crooked dartboard. She waited until they came to a stop, then dropped the darts and walked over to Zeke as they all got out of the car.

"Thought it was going to be Gabriel," Zeke said, shaking the woman's outstretched hand. There were no introductions offered.

"Ah, well, Mallory went into labor. Gabriel asked me to step in." She eyed Walker, Carlyle and Mary in quick succession, and Walker had no doubt she'd made assumptions about all of them from that quick perusal.

"I'll take the, well, it's not a car, is it? More a tin can

on wheels." The woman shrugged. "I'll pass it off a couple times. It'll end up in a barn in Nebraska if you ever want it back." She wrinkled her nose. "Can't imagine why you would."

"Thanks," Zeke said.

"Anytime." Then she fished something out of her pocket. A phone. She handed it to Zeke. "Courtesy of Wyatt. Calls you make on this can't be traced. Shay said she's poking at some Fed leads. She'll call you on this if she's got anything."

"Appreciate it." Then Zeke handed her a piece of paper. "Names and numbers for some people who've been helping. If Shay finds something and can get the FBI involved, have them give Jack Hudson a call."

She took the piece of paper and shoved it into her pocket. "Got it."

"Hell of a retirement, huh?" Zeke muttered.

The woman shrugged. "I don't mind a little downtime, but it's always nice to dip the toes in the water again. Stay safe, Daniels." She tossed Zeke the keys, gave them all a little salute, then got into Walker's car with a look of utter disgust.

She drove out of the barn door first. Zeke gestured them to get into the small SUV. Gray and bland, it looked more likely to belong to a soccer mom than a group of people trying to take down a rich, powerful senator.

In other words, perfect.

They drove out of the barn, and all the way to the town of Clearview in mostly silence. Much like last night, Zeke drove on back roads and through country fields before pulling to a stop in front of another nice cabin.

"Are y'all sure you're retired?" Walker muttered to Zeke. He didn't know what to do with his brother's other life, or all the evidence of it that Walker had never known any details about.

Zeke shrugged. "You can take the spy group away from the operative but you can't quite take the operative out of the people."

They moved inside, Zeke inputting all kinds of codes.

Then, for the next two days, they focused on the task at hand. They had phone meetings with Mary's family, Zeke had secret calls with his North Star people. They plotted, they planned.

It was strange to watch Mary work with that moment in her bedroom all those days ago in the back of his mind. When she'd been crying, falling apart. Because during this whole thing, she never seemed ruffled. Never broke down or even flinched at Zeke's hard-edged defiance when it popped up, or Carlyle's snarky commentary.

She just carefully maneuvered them forward. Together. Because it had to be done together.

Which was why it was a major concern that Carlyle was *very* quiet as they planned. In the past, Walker would have ignored that. He would have let it go, because he would have had his own secrets he was keeping.

In the present, he couldn't let that slide. It was too dangerous. Too many people were at risk, and he'd been disabused of the notion he was the grand protector who knew everything.

Carlyle had been keeping a secret since she was twelve years old. Then an even bigger one since she'd been eighteen. Walker now realized he didn't know a damn thing.

So he waited to corner her until Mary and Zeke were both occupied with the various phone calls that took up their time in the planning stages. He found Carlyle outside on the porch, sitting on the stairs.

"Missing the dogs?"

She looked back at him and smiled a little. "Yeah. You

know… Maybe when this is all over I could con Cash into giving me a job. Mary says he needs help."

Walker settled himself on the stair next to her. "Glad to hear you talking about the future."

She shrugged, but she got that look. How many times had he seen that look over the years and just assumed it was bravery covering up fear? He supposed it was, but it was deeper than that.

It was fear and bravery covering up secrets and lies.

"You're going to stick around Sunrise, aren't you?" she asked. "All that love junk."

"Yeah, all that love junk will probably keep me there."

Carlyle nodded firmly. "Good."

Walker let the quiet settle over them for a few minutes. He could feel Carlyle grow more and more uncomfortable, even as she didn't move, didn't change where she was looking out at the trees.

When Walker spoke, he kept his voice calm, even. Like Mary would. "I know we went our separate ways this last year. Tried to protect each other by staying apart, by keeping secrets and doing our own thing. It was wrong, Car."

She shrugged, somewhat jerkily. "Okay."

He didn't know how to get through to her, so maybe that was also part of why he wouldn't have tried in the past. He'd been stuck with trying to parent her and he hadn't even known how to parent himself. Older, wiser now, he could see all the places he'd failed out of simply not knowing what else to do.

Hard to beat himself up for that.

"If you're planning to self-sacrifice, you're only putting us all in danger. What we don't know *could* kill us. And I just don't mean me and Zeke. Or even Mary. There's a lot of hands in this pie now."

She looked over at him then, frowning. She was quiet

for so long he started to think maybe he'd never be able to get through to her.

"It's not your fight. He's not your father."

"But you're my sister, so it is my fight. You always will be."

She looked away, down at her hands, and he thought he saw the glimmer of tears in her eyes, but it was hard to tell with her head bowed. She swallowed audibly. "I'm going to break into his house while you and Mary meet with him."

"Carlyle—"

She looked up, eyes fierce, any trace of tears gone. "You can't change my mind. It's what I'm going to do. I'm going to find something. I have to. I wasn't going to tell you because I knew you'd try to stop me, but you can't, Walker. You won't."

He hated it, but he knew his baby sister well enough to know she was right. There was no talking her out of it, and even if he and Zeke locked her up, she'd just find a way out. A way to do exactly what she wanted. Didn't her confronting Dennison years ago prove that?

"I won't try to stop you," he said, which clearly shocked her enough not to have anything to say. "But you're going to need help."

"I... What?"

It was just what Mary had done—let Carlyle have her way, but give her the foundations and company to do it in a safer manner. "I think you should take Zeke. We can't do anything alone, and God knows Zeke has the skills. While Mary and I confront Dennison, you guys break in and see what you can find."

"You're... Did you hit your head?"

Walker laughed. "If I had my way, you wouldn't do it. But you're going to, so we might as well do it in the safest way possible."

"Zeke won't go for it."

"He will. Because if he doesn't, I'll tell him I'm calling in someone from HSS to go with you."

Carlyle's mouth slowly curved. "Well, that'd do it."

Walker nodded. Then he looked at his sister and told her what he probably should have said a long time ago—instead of high-handed declarations of protection and being the older brother.

"I love you, Car. I'd do anything to protect you, but this is dangerous enough we have to rely on each other. Trust each other. Going it alone hasn't worked in all these years, so now we're going it together. No matter what."

She hesitated. He could see it on her face, that knee-jerk recoil from relying on each other. From truly working as a team. Because it felt like teamwork meant risking the people you loved the most.

But he was coming to realize, thanks to Mary and HSS, that the benefits of it all outweighed the risks. No one could do everything on their own. He held out his hand to his sister. "Deal?"

Her mouth firmed, pushing away that hesitation in her expression. She took his outstretched hand and shook it. "It's a deal," she said.

And he had to believe she meant it.

Chapter Twenty

"I don't like it."

Mary had lost count of how many times she'd heard that over the past forty-eight hours. It was usually from Zeke, but Walker and Carlyle threw one in every once in a while.

Now it was her brother's voice over the phone. "I didn't ask for your feelings on the matter," Mary replied.

She'd told him they'd gotten an appointment set up with Senator Dennison through his secretary. And Zeke and Carlyle had prepared a plan to break into his fancy, well-secured mansion.

"I've talked to Zeke's North Star contact, this Shay woman," Jack said. "The likelihood of any federal or local law enforcement help is slim. Everyone is too afraid of Dennison."

"We're not."

Jack sighed audibly. "Mary—"

"I have to go to the meeting, Jack. We'll regroup this evening and go over what we've found. It's just an initial step," she said, though she wasn't sure she believed that.

"What Zeke and Carlyle are going to find is the inside of a jail cell if they're lucky. And you and Walker could be right there with them."

"We'll cross that bridge when we come to it."

He groaned, which was very un-Jack-like, so she knew

he was at the end of his rope. But she couldn't change their plans. "I'll talk to you soon." She hesitated, because it was not something they said casually, but… Well, she was very well aware she was walking into danger no matter how many precautions they took. "I love you."

"Jeez, Mary, I—"

But she hung up on him, because she knew she'd worried him with those words and she couldn't focus on Jack and his feelings when she had a scary meeting to go to.

She returned to the living room and handed Zeke the untraceable phone. He put it in his pocket.

"You guys should get going."

Walker nodded but pulled Zeke and Carlyle into a three-way hug like he had back at the cabin when Zeke and Carlyle had shown up. But this time, Walker pulled Mary into the little huddle, as well. Their heads were together, their arms were around each other.

A team. A family.

"No unnecessary risks," Walker said firmly. "No self-sacrifice. We get what we can get, and we leave the rest. There's always tomorrow if we don't get what we need today. We have to agree on that, trust that. We have to."

Zeke nodded, then Carlyle. When Walker looked at Mary, she nodded too. Then they pulled apart and collected everything they needed.

Mary got the messenger bag with all the things she would usually carry if she was questioning someone. A tablet, a notebook, a list of typed-up questions about the situation at hand. She was prepared and ready just as if this was an average HSS questioning.

Too bad she didn't usually conduct those. And too bad it wasn't. This was far from usual, because Carlyle and Zeke would be attempting to break into a well-secured house while she and Walker faced down a potential murderer. A rich, powerful murderer.

She walked outside with the Daniels siblings. First, Walker dropped Zeke and Carlyle off at a bus stop—where they'd take a bus to a meet up with one of Zeke's North Star people and pick up a new car. While they did that, Mary and Walker drove deeper into town, toward the library, the neutral meeting point that had been arranged with Dennison's secretary.

They drove in silence, both too lost in their own thoughts and worries to come up with conversation. All those worries doubled when they pulled into the library parking lot. The library was supposed to be a public meeting place, with people and witnesses.

But the parking lot was empty.

Walker's frown got progressively deeper as he pulled into a parking space.

"I don't like this," Walker said, staring up at what appeared to be the empty building.

And though she'd heard that a lot over the past few days, this was the first time she fully agreed. "Me either."

Walker studied the surroundings. She could see him filing things away. She also knew he was armed. In her bag, she had a recording device, and a little panic button that would send a text to everyone saying they needed help.

They had so much help, there was really no need to be this afraid. Or so she tried to tell herself.

"We still have to go in," Walker said grimly. "We have to make sure he's here, or Carlyle and Zeke are in trouble."

Mary nodded. They got out of the car and met at the hood. Walker took her hand. They weren't supposed to look like people who had anything more than a working relationship, but Mary knew he needed the connection.

And so did she.

They moved carefully up to the library front doors. Mary tried not to hesitate when she saw that the doors were open and there were people waiting in the lobby. Not a public kind of people, but Senator Connor Dennison himself. He was flanked by two large men in black, no doubt his security detail.

Walker squeezed her hand, then released it as they stepped through the open doors, which closed behind them with what sounded like a very menacing *click*.

"Dennison. This isn't quite what we anticipated," Walker said. His voice was strong. Unafraid. "We did say somewhere *public*."

"Yes, you did. But you want to talk about things that are...let's say, private. So I rented out this place so we could have some of the required privacy." He smiled brightly, as if this was the most reasonable course of action in the world.

"You rented out the public library?"

Dennison didn't so much as flinch or blink. He turned a dark gaze to Mary. "You must be Ms. Hudson. You're the one who has questions for me?"

"We both have questions, Senator. I'm just helping facilitate Mr. Beck's quest for the truth." Mary was proud of how businesslike she sounded.

"Quest for truth." Dennison threw his head back and laughed. "That's an interesting way of putting it. And since we're talking about truth, let's stop dancing around it." All that cold mirth left his expression and he stopped laughing and smiling.

"Your sister has been a thorn in my side long enough," he said, glaring at Walker. "You were kind enough to deliver the one thing she cares about right to my lap." The man smiled, but it was a chilling, soulless kind of smile. "I knew if I waited long enough you three would mess up your own lives."

One of the guards stepped forward and roughly grabbed Mary. She could see the other guard had done the same to Walker, and he was definitely not going without a fight.

So Mary fought. She kicked, she scratched, she punched.

But then a gun was pressed to her temple and she stilled completely.

WALKER FELT HIS entire body seize up in utter terror. There was nothing stopping Dennison from pulling the trigger. He'd rented out this damn library, and it didn't matter that it was broad daylight outside, he could kill her.

And there was nothing Walker could do.

Had they really been this stupid?

"Take him," Dennison said, jerking his chin toward the back. "If he causes a problem, make sure to let me know." Dennison used the hand not pressing a gun to Mary's head to cup her chin. "For every fight," he told Walker, "your friend here gets punished."

Walker was still frozen, and when the guard jerked him forward, he had no choice but to go. He couldn't call Dennison's bluff when the man had a gun to Mary's head, because there was a very real possibility there was no bluff.

Walker was led deeper into the library, then down some stairs and into a back room full of boxes. He didn't fight—he would, when the moment was right, but right now he knew Mary would pay the price for that fight.

So, when they shoved him into the room, he went. When they took his gun, he let them. One held him against the wall and the other landed a hard punch right to his gut, and he bent over but he didn't fight back. They landed blows, one after the other, and Walker simply took them.

Blood trickled down his face from various places, and still he let them.

After a few particularly vicious punches to the kidneys,

one of the guards gave him a little shake. "Fight back, you idiot."

Since it seemed to be what they wanted, Walker only shook his head. "No." He tensed, waiting for more blows to rain down.

Instead, they dropped him and he fell to his knees. He struggled to breathe through the pain. Had to fight to focus on what was next. How to survive this—because that psychopath had Mary.

Inexplicably the two guards just left. Oh, Walker was sure he was locked in the room, but this didn't make any damn sense. Still he managed to get to his feet and cross over to the door, just to make sure.

Yeah, locked.

He wiped the blood dripping off his chin with the back of his hand and studied the room. He ignored the pain and kept his brain engaged, moving boxes, looking for any way out or any weapon. Time stretched out until he lost any sense of it. He had no idea how long it had been when the door opened again.

Walker got in a fighting stance though his body throbbed. He'd fight his way out if given the chance.

But it wasn't the guards, it was Dennison himself. Walker's body went cold. Too many terrible possibilities worked through him at seeing Dennison enter alone. Still, he didn't speak. Couldn't.

The senator's eyes were cold staring at Walker, maybe cataloging the damage the guards had done to him.

Walker didn't ask about Mary. He felt like that's what Dennison wanted, and worse, Walker couldn't think about what might have happened to her. Not until he had a chance to get to her.

He eyed the distance between him and the senator, gauging his ability to ram into Dennison and escape. But no doubt the guards were waiting right outside the door.

"My guards said you refused to fight back."

"What's the point?"

Dennison clearly didn't like this, though Walker couldn't begin to understand why.

"Once your sister and brother come to save you, as they no doubt will, I'll wipe the three of you out," Dennison said after a while. "It'll look like a tragic accident. Your brother saw combat, didn't he? Traumatic brain injuries do such a terrible number on people. He got a little drunk, went a little crazy and shot his siblings. Then in a fit of despair he killed himself."

"Bummer," Walker replied sarcastically. No reason to play into Dennison's little game, even if it left him feeling sick to his stomach.

"Don't you want to know what's going to become of the woman you brought into the fray?"

"No."

"Ah, well, don't worry. I have more long-range plans for her before death."

Walker had to work very hard not to react. It was clear that's what Dennison wanted. Him to be on the attack. Him to give something away.

But it was the senator who'd given something away. The fact that everyone Walker loved was still alive.

Maybe they were in danger, but they were alive, and as long as they were, he'd do everything to stay alive too.

Chapter Twenty-One

Mary stood in the middle of a strangely opulent bedroom. She had expected a lot of things when Dennison had forced her into his car at gunpoint. Being driven to his mansion was not one of them. Being taken to a very nice bedroom even less of one. Especially since no one had hurt her or said anything to her. Just led her here like she was a guest.

Of course, they'd taken her bag, searched her and locked her in. Was Walker as lucky?

She couldn't think about that. She had to think about how to get away. Were Zeke and Carlyle, even now, somewhere in this house looking for evidence? Could she get to them?

And if she could, could they all get out and get to Walker?

He hadn't been in the car with her, and if she let her mind go to where he was being held, it went to too many terrible places to name. There was nothing to be done except get herself out of this mess. Because while she might be safe enough right now, at the end of the day, there was no plan for her that could be positive. Connor Dennison had shown his hand. He'd been the one to hold a gun to her head and essentially kidnap her.

There was no way he just let her go when he'd have to face the consequences.

She decided not to think about any of the reasons he might want to keep her alive for the time being. None of them were good, but all of them gave her the opportunity to escape.

So she searched the room. Carefully, quietly. Pausing every so often to listen for footsteps outside the door. She looked out the window, but all she saw were thick leaves—a tree or very tall bush, she supposed, hiding whatever went on in this bedroom. She'd been walked up at least one flight of stairs, so she definitely wasn't on the ground floor.

She was about to test the window to see if it would open when she heard the doorknob turn. She whirled around to face it, took a few steps away from the window and clasped her hands together in front of her.

She didn't know what she'd be up against, so all she knew to lead with was her usual contained demeanor.

Dennison himself stepped into the room. He closed the door behind him. Fear twined through her, but he didn't have a gun. At least in his hands. Who knew what the suit jacket he wore hid.

He didn't say anything at first, just studied her, the kind of perusal that had her tightening the grip of her hands and fighting the urge to shrink in on herself.

"You seem like the kind of woman who might be reasonable, Mary Hudson. And I could use a reasonable woman."

Mary worked as hard as she ever had to keep her polite smile in place. "It's hard to be reasonable when you've had a gun pointed at your head and been kidnapped."

Connor smiled. She supposed if she took away all the fear, she might understand why someone could find that smile charming, but she only saw the cruelty behind it.

He stepped forward and held out a phone—*her* phone that had been in her bag. "Let's give reason a try. First, I want you to call your family. Tell them you had an informative meeting with me and you'll be in touch in a few days. Can you do that?"

Mary's mind raced for the right answer. Fight? Go along with him? She really had no idea. She knew Walker and his siblings would fight, but that wasn't her strong suit. Why not lean into her strengths?

So she forced herself to smile. As if he was a client. As if it was her job to help him. "Of course."

He touched the screen of her phone and held it out to her—not so she could take it, but so she could type in her passcode. He watched her enter in the numbers, which was probably a bad thing, but in the moment Mary didn't know how to avoid it.

"Now call home, Mary. Tell them you'll be a few days and not to worry."

She tried to take the phone, but he clucked his tongue and held firm. "On speaker, of course."

Mary didn't let that make her falter. She just followed instructions and hoped to God whoever answered didn't give anything away. Or believe her, for that matter. She called the home landline, hoping no one picked up and she could maybe just leave a message.

But Anna answered on the second ring.

"Anna. Hi."

"Hey. Everything okay?"

"Yes, everything is fine," Mary said, keeping her voice devoid of any inflection. She didn't look at Dennison. She just stared hard at the phone. "I've met with Senator Dennison. Everything went as expected. We should be back home in a few days."

"That's it?" Anna replied, somewhat incredulously.

Mary looked up at Connor. He gave her a little nod, so she swallowed. "Yes. We're going to be pretty busy, so I may not call in a day or two and I didn't want you to worry."

"I can barely hear you. Are you on speaker or something?"

"Yes. Yes, I'm driving. I'll call again in a few days, all right?"

"Okay. Be safe. Call if you need anything."

"I will. Goodbye."

Connor hit the end button and tucked the phone away in his inside suit pocket. Mary didn't know if Anna had picked up on anything being wrong as it was highly irregular for her not to want to check in. There was no reason for her to be driving on speakerphone.

Even if Anna had thought something was wrong, what would they do with something so innocuous? Come to Colorado?

Be too late?

No, she wouldn't think like that.

"Excellent work," Connor said. If she'd been in just about any other situation she might have been warmed by such an enthusiastic compliment. But his smile had her fighting the urge to step back. To protect herself.

He moved closer. "We might just make an excellent team, Ms. Hudson." He reached out and touched her cheek. She couldn't resist the urge this time—she jerked away from his touch.

He sighed heavily, like she'd disappointed him greatly. Then without warning his hand shot out, backhanding her cheek hard enough that she stumbled, catching herself on a dresser so she didn't fall.

He leaned in close, eyes blazing with an incongruous fury to the words he spoke. "You need a few lessons in how to deal with your superior, Ms. Hudson."

He moved forward this time, no creepy, gentle touches. His hand was on her throat, and Mary frantically searched her brain for any of the self-defense maneuvers she'd been taught.

He leaned in close. "Say, 'Yes, sir, Senator Dennison.'"

Mary swallowed at the terror and bile threatening to choke her. "Yes, sir, Senator Dennison," she managed, though it was weak and scratchy.

He gave her a hard shove and this time she did fall to the floor. But at least his hands weren't on her any longer. And he was striding out of the room, slamming the door behind him.

Mary gave herself a minute to regroup, there on the floor. To slow her breathing, to wipe away the tears that had filled her eyes. That was scary, but she was still in one piece. She was still alive, and maybe—just maybe—Anna had picked up on the fact that she wasn't herself.

Granted, Mary didn't know what her siblings could do, but it was a hope to hold on to, something she could use to get through this.

Gingerly, she picked herself up. She looked around, her eyes landing on the window.

All those weeks ago, when she'd first laid eyes on Walker Daniels, they'd escaped out a window.

Now she'd have to figure out a way to do the same.

IT TOOK HOURS. Careful, tedious hours. She pulled the bed apart, took anything that wouldn't be necessarily missed, then remade it with the coverlet and pillows. She moved it all into the little en suite bathroom. Since there was no door to the hall in here, she locked herself inside just in case someone came in.

It was like something out of a ridiculous movie, but she didn't let that stop her. She tied together the sheets, the little hand towels, the liner of the shower curtain. Whatever worked that wouldn't be immediately noticed.

If she fell to her death because her makeshift rope didn't work, she figured it was better than the alternative.

She heard something—likely someone coming into her

room. She shoved everything behind the shower curtain, flushed the toilet. She looked around for a mirror, but there was none. She washed her hands and swallowed down her nerves before wiping her hands on her pants.

She stepped out of the bathroom to find Dennison again. There was a tray of food and candles on the little desk in the corner. He'd dimmed the lights, and the candles flickered like terrifying spirits of doom.

In another setting, with another man, it might have been seen as romantic, but there was only an ever-worsening fear that there was no way to escape this. And *this* was worse than she'd feared.

"I'm sure you're starving. Sit. Eat."

She wasn't sure she'd be able to stomach a bite, but she also knew his words were not a request. Stiffly, she moved over to the desk and sat. He moved, too, standing right next to her as she surveyed the food.

He watched her every move, and it worried her. Had he tampered with the food? Still, she picked up a fork, not sure what else to do. Claim food allergies? Stubbornly refuse? She eyed the tray itself. Could she upend it in his face and run away?

"No need to worry about the food." He reached down, picked a little potato off the plate and popped it into his mouth. He washed it down with whatever was in the glass— maybe some kind of wine. "I'm not going to poison you, Mary. I want you to work for me."

She blinked up at him. "Why would you want me to do that?"

"Many reasons. I have a need for good staff who can be trusted or blackmailed. I even thought about using those Daniels brothers. They have the skills to be excellent... muscle," he said, as if thinking over the appropriate descriptor. "But unfortunately for them, they just don't suit. And it seems I might finally have a chance to eradicate them both."

Mary couldn't even come up with a response. But she didn't have to. Dennison droned on and on about opportunities.

"You see, I like the people who work for me to owe me." Then he smiled down at her, and she had to pretend like it didn't make her skin crawl. She swallowed a small bite of food even though she couldn't taste anything.

She smiled at him, though she wasn't sure she was a good enough actor to make it come off as polite. Maybe he was delusional enough to assume it was. "And what do I owe you?"

"Your life, of course. And now that I've done my research, your family's lives, as well." He pulled out her phone, angled the screen so she could see, then brought up her pictures. He swiped through until he found one of Izzy cuddling a puppy.

Mary couldn't hold her smile in place, but she said nothing. She didn't move. Maybe she didn't breathe.

"Cute," he said. "I wouldn't kill her, I don't think. It's best to teach them young, you know."

Mary refused to ask him what he meant by that. It seemed exactly what he wanted, and while she was desperately trying to play along, there were some lines she didn't know how to cross, even in pretend.

"But the rest of them would be easily wiped out. That fire investigator your sister's married to got a little too fast and loose with his pyromania and *whoosh*. It'll take some time, just like the Daniels brothers did, but it would be done. You can either work for me in the interim or be tortured by me." His smile widened. "I'm happy with either eventuality, of course. I'm flexible like that. So, it's your choice."

Mary carefully set her fork down. She folded her hands in her lap. "I can't say it feels like much of a choice."

Connor laughed, then took her by the arm and pulled her to her feet. "You sound like my wife, Mary. Unfortunate. *She* has her uses—deep pockets and deep roots. You? You're a toy. At best." His hand came to her face again and he ran his fingers through her hair. "I don't always break my toys, Mary, but I will if you don't cooperate."

His hands slid down her neck, then over her arms, his fingers curling around them in a tight, painful grip. "The people who work for me do whatever I say, whenever I say." His fingers dug into her arms so hard it would no doubt leave bruises.

She was shaking now. She didn't know how to get out of this. He was bigger than her, stronger than her. She had no weapons. No exits. She could fight and maybe do some damage, but she wouldn't be able to get away.

Still, she'd hardly just stand here and take it. She was about to knee his groin when a chime sounded. Connor paused for a moment, though his cold gaze never left hers. After a moment, another chime, then he stepped back. He took his phone out of his pocket, looked at the screen, then scowled.

He said nothing. Just collected his tray of food and candles and left.

Mary nearly collapsed with relief. Tears began to fall, but she didn't acknowledge them. There was no time. There was only trying to get out. And if she fell and broke her neck, it was better than the alternative.

Once he was gone, she ran to the bathroom and got her makeshift rope. She tied one end to the bedpost and brought the rest to the window. She ripped the coverlet off the bed and wrapped it around her arm over and over until it created enough padding against breaking glass.

He'd left in a hurry, so she assumed he wouldn't hear, but if he did, she didn't care. If he came in here, she'd fight him with shards of glass. She'd jump out the window. She'd do *whatever*. But she wasn't standing here taking anything anymore.

She grabbed the lamp off the desk, ripped it from the outlet. She wrapped the base in some coverlet fabric, too, to hopefully muffle the noise.

Then she rammed it into the window. The glass shattered, but the coverlet softened some of the noise. She didn't wait to see if anyone came running. She just kept hitting the lamp against the glass, making a bigger and bigger hole until she knew she could get through it. Her hand throbbed, she could barely breathe, but the gauzy haze of fear made everything kind of surreal and she thought of little else than the next step.

Throw the makeshift rope over the sill. It wouldn't get her all the way down, but it didn't matter.

Nothing mattered except getting out of here.

She didn't look down, just held on to the rope and climbed out. She didn't question whether the knots were slipping. She just worked on shimmying her way down, holding on to whatever branches or pieces of the outside wall that might help distribute her weight.

It was dark, and the rustling of the leaves as she moved through them made her nervous. Everything made her nervous. She had no idea how far she'd gone when she realized things were slipping. The makeshift rope wasn't going to hold.

Oh, God. She was going to fall. She wracked her brain for anything she'd ever learned about how to fall without breaking a bone. Surely Palmer and Anna had discussed how to be thrown from a bull before.

"Just drop," she heard someone say—but it was in a

hissed whisper, not a sharp demand. "I'll catch you. I've got you. You're not far."

It was Zeke's voice. She couldn't seem to manage to look down to verify it. Her limbs were shaking, and she was hanging there, slowly going down.

"Damn it, Mary, drop."

She had no choice. She let go and fell. It was a short fall, on that he hadn't been lying. And he did catch her—somehow. It was a little painful. A lot jarring.

But she didn't crash to the ground and she supposed that was something.

"There. I've got you." He put her down on her feet, but she couldn't quite let go.

She held on tight, the relief making her weak. "You're okay. Thank God." She pulled back, looked wildly around. Carlyle was there.

"They know we're here," Zeke said disgustedly. "Not where yet, but they know."

"Where's Walker?" Carlyle demanded.

"I don't know," Mary said. "They separated us. He didn't come to this house, I don't think. But I put that tracker on him this morning. Dennison has my phone, but if we can get a hold of my family, they should be able to get into the tracker and tell us where he is."

"Let's go." Zeke kept her hand in his, and she realized he held Carlyle's with his other one. They stepped forward into the grass, but then Zeke pulled them both to a stop, and that's when Mary noticed that lights were flashing on. Big, bright security lights. One by one.

"We've got to get out of here without them finding us first," Zeke muttered, jerking them all into one of the large shrubs.

Chapter Twenty-Two

Walker had gone through every possible escape avenue. He was dizzy with hunger, shaking with rage and fear, and there was no way out of this basement room. If he thought there was any chance of it doing anything, he might have beat his hands bloody to get out.

Instead, he had to stand around and wait. Wait for Connor Dennison to kill him.

No. No. There had to be a way to fight. Had to be. So he went through everything in the room, and began setting up some kind of trap. Something that would catch Dennison off guard.

If Dennison had guards with him… Well, Walker had fought off more than one man before. Better than just accepting death anyway. So he did what he could to stack boxes in such a way they could come down on an unsuspecting person who might enter thinking they were the only one with a weapon.

Walker worked on finding a good position on the other side that might take Dennison or his guards by surprise. But before he could decide exactly how to position himself, he heard footsteps. After not more than a few seconds, he heard someone shout.

"Stand back."

Walker stared at the door, more than a little confused.

But he stood back. "Okay," he shouted, though his voice was raw from disuse and lack of water.

A loud *boom* echoed through the building, and then the door fell open. On the other side of the dust and debris were three men, with guns drawn. They studied the room, growing expressions of confusion on their faces.

"Just you?" one asked pointedly.

They weren't the senator's guards. They looked like law enforcement, with bulletproof vests and tactical gear. "Yeah. Just me. Who are you?"

The man in front pulled out a badge. "FBI. We got an anonymous tip that there was a human trafficking ring going on in the basement of this library. Who are you?"

An anonymous tip. That had to be the Hudsons or maybe Zeke's North Star Group. It obviously wasn't *true*, so he considered offering an alias. Then he decided against it. Finding Mary was more important than any lie or complication. "My name is Walker Daniels. I was tossed in here by Senator Connor Dennison. He kidnapped Mary Hudson, or his men did. I didn't see. We were separated."

"We have two of his guards in custody. Follow me, Mr. Daniels."

He was led out of the library basement, up the stairs and outside into the dark night where a small contingent of law enforcement officers huddled around cars.

"It was Senator Dennison," Walker told the agent again. "He's who locked me down there. We've got to get to the woman he kidnapped. Mary Hudson."

"I heard you," the agent said. "First, do you need medical attention, Mr. Daniels?"

"No, I need to find Mary."

The FBI agent didn't seem to pay him any mind, just waved over a man in a suit. "I'm sorry, Mr. Daniels, but we'll need to take you into the station to ask you some questions. We'll get to the bottom of this whole thing."

The man who'd been waved over said something in low tones, and the two men began to converse. Then they walked over to a third agent, clearly trying to keep Walker from hearing what they were saying.

They were help—they had to be help—but there was no sense of urgency. Of *movement*. Didn't they understand that Mary was in danger? Walker looked around at the dark night. He couldn't go to some station and answer questions. He had to get to Mary.

"Daniels."

Walker looked around, saw a man standing in the shadows. Walker didn't recognize him, but he took a few steps toward the man while the suits discussed something important, or what they deemed important.

The man held out a hand as Walker approached.

"Granger Macmillan. North Star. Former North Star anyway. If you don't want to go with the Feds, you can come with me."

"Where are you going?"

"To help your brother."

"Then I'm going with you." And Walker didn't bother to look back.

Though it was the middle of the night, the entire yard was flooded with light. Mary stood with Carlyle and Zeke, huddled behind thick shrubbery. It might be hiding them now, but Mary knew their safe harbor wouldn't last. They'd be found. And then what?

"What's the plan?" Carlyle whispered.

Zeke said nothing. Mary didn't know if he was still formulating a plan or was really that concerned about being quiet, but she squeezed Carlyle's hand in hers as a kind of reassurance.

This wasn't ideal, but at least they weren't locked up anywhere. There was still a chance they'd get out of this. "We should move along the shrubs, for as long as they go," she proposed.

Zeke shook his head. "We'll make too much noise."

"Dogs," Carlyle whispered. "Listen! They're sending dogs to sniff us out."

Mary listened to the rustle of shrubs, the muffled sound of men giving orders far off in the distance. And yes, the telltale sound of dogs and dog commands.

"They'd be trained dogs," Mary said. "Carlyle, has Cash taught you any of his whistles?"

"I don't know that I remember them, but I can try."

"You whistle to get them to bark. When they start barking, we run. It'll cover the noise at least for a little bit, and it might create confusion," Mary said.

"And if they don't start barking?" Zeke asked.

"We run anyway. Better to run than be surrounded here." She thought of Connor's hands on her and fought off a shudder.

Zeke sighed. The kind of sigh that was reluctant agreement because there were no other options.

"All right. But you better be ready to run your asses off and—" He reached out, gripping them both hard. "Did you hear that?"

"What?"

Mary strained to hear something, anything. A faint kind of whistle, maybe?

"That's backup," Zeke whispered, and he was clearly happy with this turn of events. "All right. Carlyle, you make the dogs bark and you two run through the shrubs for the woods. You hear a whistle that's not your own, you run toward it. It's help."

"We're not leaving you here, Zeke," Carlyle said, clutching her brother's arms.

"Mary, take her and—"

Mary shook her head. "No. We don't leave anyone behind. We run, you run. That's the only deal."

Zeke swore under his breath. "Fine. But if they start shooting, I'm shooting back. You two keep running. I'm the only one with a gun."

"Zeke—"

"I promise I won't stay behind, Car. I promise."

Carlyle's exhale was shaky, but she agreed.

"Ready?" Zeke asked her.

Carlyle nodded, then whistled. Nothing happened at first, and Mary's heart sank. Fear began to clog her lungs, but then...

One dog yipped. Then another. Carlyle whistled again and the dogs began to howl.

"All right. Go!" Zeke commanded.

Mary grasped Carlyle's hand and they ran. Zeke was right behind them. Mary heard more howling, getting closer, but they kept running through the shrubs. There was no time to feel any sense of victory. No victory to enjoy until they were out of this mess.

A shot sounded as they reached the trees. "Just keep running," Zeke instructed, before shooting back.

Mary tried not to flinch at every shot, but as they cleared the shrubs and got into the trees, away from all those bright lights and detection, it got harder and harder to run. They had to slow so as not to fall over the exposed roots and rocks.

Carlyle stumbled, and Mary somehow managed to hold on to her arm tight enough to keep them from going down.

But then a gunshot exploded in front of them, and she heard the telltale sounds of something falling with a thud. Mary turned to see Zeke hit his knees. She jerked Carlyle back to Zeke and they huddled around him.

"Just my shoulder," he said through gritted teeth. He tried to get to his feet, but they all froze as a figure stepped out of the shadows, the dark that she'd thought had been their safety.

Senator Dennison held a gun in one hand, a flashlight in the other. Carlyle and Mary moved in front of Zeke as if to protect him, though it would take nothing for Connor to shoot them all.

"Thought you'd get the FBI involved? Thought you'd thwart *me*?" Dennison laughed. "You'll never beat me. No one will *ever* beat me."

Mary reached behind her, keeping her gaze on Connor. Zeke had a gun around here somewhere. She only had to get it while Dennison went on and on about how much smarter than them he was.

Then a twig snapped behind Dennison and he whirled around, giving her the opportunity to search for the gun with her eyes. She spotted it on the ground and moved to grab it when she saw Zeke pick it up and hand it to Carlyle. She raised her arm, ready to shoot, but two men stepped into view behind Dennison.

Walker. He stood there in front of her. Alive and well, along with a man she didn't recognize. Each held a gun pointed straight at the senator.

"Drop it," the stranger said to Dennison.

Carlyle had Zeke's gun pointed at Dennison's back, Walker and this man at his front.

"Now," Walker said flatly.

Dennison began a slow crouch, as if to put the gun down on the ground. "You think you're all so clever? I didn't kill your mother. I didn't kill anyone. All I had to do was pay Don to do my dirty work. And when he couldn't keep his mouth shut about that, I had him killed too. You won't be able to pin murder on me. You won't be able to pin *anything* on me. There's no evidence. I made sure of that."

Zeke reached into his pocket, grunting in pain, pulled out a little device and played Connor's words back for him. "I don't know about that."

Connor whirled, but by turning his back on Walker and the stranger, he gave them the opportunity to grab him from behind, wrestle the gun out of his hand.

"There's no getting out of this now." Carlyle smirked at him while Walker and the man held him still. "I knew if I gave you enough time and rope, you'd hang yourself." She cocked the trigger.

Mary held her breath, expecting Walker or even the stranger to intervene. But they stood there and let her do what she needed to do.

Carlyle held the gun pointed at her father's head. Mary herself almost stepped forward. Maybe her brothers thought it was justice but she didn't. She couldn't let this happen.

"I can't wait to watch this trial play out. To watch all your dreams go up in smoke," Carlyle said, though she kept the gun trained on him. "I'll be first in line to testify."

"I'll die first."

"If you do, it'll be by your own hand. Not mine."

She didn't lower the gun, but she stood there, glaring into his cold eyes. Then law enforcement ran up the hill with their own weapons drawn.

It was chaotic, at best. Walker and his new friend were yelling about getting Zeke medical treatment. Mary had to help Carlyle talk her way out of having been one of the people holding a gun at someone.

Mary tried to reach Walker in the crowd, but she'd only

caught glimpses of him. There were questions. Being moved from the woods to the front of the property where Dennison's staff were lined up, talking to different law enforcement officers.

She was led by an FBI agent toward this lineup, while Carlyle was led toward an ambulance with flashing lights. Inside, Walker crouched beside Zeke, who lay on a stretcher.

"Wait," Carlyle said to the guy leading her in the opposite direction. "She needs to come with me to the hospital."

"Family only."

"She's family," Carlyle said stubbornly, jerking away from the agent and striding over to where Mary stood with a different agent.

"You can't all go in the ambulance," the agent told her.

"Then someone needs to drive Mary and me to the hospital while Walker and Zeke ride in the ambulance."

Mary forced herself to smile, to reach out and give Carlyle a little squeeze. "Car, it's okay."

"No, it isn't. She's coming with me. And one of you is taking me to the hospital. Because if you'd done your jobs about five minutes faster, my brother wouldn't have been shot."

Mary watched as the agents exchanged tired, irritated looks. But they didn't argue with Carlyle any longer.

"Come on," the agent said, and Mary and Carlyle were led to a cop car, where an officer was tasked with driving them to the hospital.

Mary was moving purely on fumes. By the time they got to the hospital, nothing fully felt real. She got the impression Carlyle was having the same reaction, so they kind of clutched and leaned on each other as they were led to a waiting room.

And then Mary saw Walker, practically prowling the small room. He stopped short when they entered. Then he moved over so quickly she wasn't sure how it had happened and pulled her close. He didn't say anything, just held on. Mary pressed her forehead to his shoulder and inhaled.

He was okay. Whole and in one piece. Zeke wasn't, but he would be okay. He had to be.

"How's Zeke?" Carlyle asked, a lot of her bravery having faded into a quavering voice.

"Good enough. They'll give me an update soon, but there wasn't any life-or-death concern." His voice was rough, and she could feel a kind of tremor inside him. Likely not just because of emotion, but because he, too, had been hurt.

"Walker, has a doctor looked at you?"

"I'm good," he said, which did not answer the question. She looked up at him, ready to argue because he was bruised and bloody, but something cold and furious passed over his expression as his gaze landed on her throat.

No doubt Connor had left bruises.

"I'm good too," she said, using his same tone and raising an eyebrow at him, as if daring him to argue with her when *she* had not argued with him.

"Mary..."

She shook her head. Even though she didn't know exactly what he wanted to say, she knew it didn't matter. "We're all okay."

He let out a shaky breath, then led them both over to some chairs. They kind of collapsed in a heap—Mary on one side of Walker, Carlyle on the other. He kept his arms around both of them as they sat.

No one said anything. What was there to say? It was over. *Over.*

There was only one thing to mention.

"When Zeke gets out, we'll all go home. He can recuperate on the ranch. We'll take good care of him," Mary said firmly. "The Hudsons have had lots of practice in that department. You'll come home and we'll take care of everything."

Walker looked over at her. She couldn't quite read his expression, but his mouth curved ever so slightly, then he leaned forward and kissed her temple. "Yeah, we'll all go home."

She didn't miss the way his voice got rougher at that word. That thing he hadn't had in so long. Tears stung her eyes, but she didn't let them fall.

Because she was going to give them all the best home there ever was. Forever.

Carlyle nodded, and they sat there, holding on to each other, ready to go home.

Together.

Epilogue

It took a few days to get back to the ranch. Zeke needed an overnight stay in the hospital and the questions from the FBI were endless. Walker tried not to mind. Whatever could be done to keep Connor Dennison behind bars he would do.

Luckily, Dennison was even shadier than they'd anticipated, and they weren't the only ones trying to take him down. The Feds had just needed a needle that broke the camel's back—and the help Zeke's former North Star group had given made all the difference.

There was always the chance Dennison's fancy lawyers would get him off for some things, but the sheer amount of wrongdoing he'd been involved in would likely keep him locked up for a long time.

Even his wife had come forward with charges of decades of abuse. No, even his money and influence wouldn't get him out of the mess he'd made for himself.

Walker had insisted Mary go home, and he was sure he only got her to go before him by asking her to get a room ready for Zeke. His brother would be fine, but he'd need some help and care while his gunshot wound healed.

There was no arguing that Mary would be the one over-seeing that process.

Mary. He still wasn't over the details of what Dennison

had done to her. That would take…time. It would take a hell of a lot of time to get over all of this.

But they'd do it together, so he couldn't wait to get home and get started.

He'd had his SUV delivered to him so he could drive Zeke from Colorado to the Hudson Ranch with some room. Zeke was currently stretched out in the back while Carlyle practically bounced in the passenger seat the closer they got to Sunrise.

And home.

Walker wasn't sure when he'd started to see it that way— but it was sometime before Mary had said it in the hospital the other day. Maybe in those first moments he'd come to the ranch. It had always felt right.

Or maybe that was just Mary herself.

"How much longer?" Carlyle whined, like the thirteen-year-old she never fully got to be.

"Not long," Walker replied, feeling the same frustrating anticipation coiled inside him.

He glanced at his sister. She hadn't said she would yet, but he knew she'd take the dog training assistant job Cash offered. As for Walker himself, he figured he had the skills to be a decent HSS team member, and he could learn how to be a ranch hand if needed.

Zeke would have to make his own choices, but Walker hoped his brother would join HSS too. Do a little good in the world for other people.

But none of what would come mattered when he pulled into the Hudson Ranch, and Mary was waiting for them on the porch.

He nearly leaped from the car, but there were a swarm of Hudsons—to help Zeke, to get their bags. Mary gave out orders, and everyone jumped to follow them. Zeke grumbled a little, but Walker figured he'd earned a grumble or two.

Then finally everyone was inside, except him.

And Mary.

They stood on the porch, facing each other. He wanted to pull her into his arms and just hold on for a hundred years.

And that was just it.

He wanted years. And years and years. That's all he could seem to think about in this moment. He didn't know what else to say to her but "Marry me."

She didn't look shocked, or appalled, thank God. He didn't have a ring or a plan, just a feeling. And she stood there, one of those polite smiles on her face, but her eyes shone.

"I always thought I'd have to know someone at least a year before I agreed to marry them," she said carefully. Oh, so carefully.

"I can wait." And he could. Marriage was just a piece of paper anyway. As long as Mary loved him and was by his side, being married didn't matter. He smiled at her because he was home and that's what mattered.

He reached out for her, wound his arm around her waist and felt a tension inside of him ease. It was really all over, and she was here. Within reach. When he went to bed tonight, she'd be right next to him. Loving him.

"You got any coffee?" he asked, because he was dead on his feet and to get to that point, he'd need some caffeine.

But before he could move for the door to open it, she moved into his way. "That's just it, Walker." She looked up at him, put her hand on his cheek. "With you, I don't want to wait. I want to marry you."

It took a minute—he blamed it on exhaustion. *I want to marry you.* He grinned down at her.

"Soon," she added, emphatically.

Soon. He laughed and went ahead and gave in to impulse and lifted her up.

"Soon sounds good." Then he pressed his mouth to hers.

Because she *was* home. His. And he was finally, fully and permanently right where he wanted to be.

"Oh, my God, you guys, get a room!" Carlyle shouted through the window at them. But there was humor in her tone and it made Mary laugh, so Walker laughed too.

Because he hadn't had a home for a very long time, but Mary had given him one. And that was worth everything it had taken to get here.

* * * * *